MOTHERS OF THE PROPHETS
SERIES

Abigail Howe Young
"Nabby"

MOTHERS OF THE PROPHETS
SERIES

Abigail Howe Young

"Nabby"

By
Lisa J. Peck

Rebecca,
Have a great
Mother's Day!
Lisa J. Peck

CFI
Springville, Utah

ISBN: 1-55517-790-5
e. 1

Published by CFI
An Imprint of Cedar Fort Inc.
www.cedarfort.com

Distributed by:

Cover illustration by Mary Shaffer
Cover design by Nicole Shaffer
Cover design © 2004 by Lyle Mortimer

Printed in the United States of America
10 9 8 7 6 5 4 3 2 1
Printed on acid-free paper

Library of Congress Cataloging-in-Publication Data

Peck, Lisa J.
  Abigail Howe Young / by Lisa J. Peck.
      p. cm. -- (Mothers of the prophets series)
  Includes bibliographical references.
  ISBN 1-55517-790-5 (alk. paper)
  1. Young, Abigail Howe, 1766-1815--Fiction. 2. Young, Brigham,
1801-1877--Family--Fiction. 3. Mothers and sons--Fiction. 4. Mormon
women--Fiction. I. Title. II. Series.

  PS3566.E2517A64 2004
  813'.54--dc22

                    2004020357

Dedication

To Madeline, my passionate, loving, adventure.

Acknowledgments

A special thank-you to Susan Evans McCloud for her skillful editor's eye and historical expertise.

Chapter 1

Amazing Grace

Amazing grace, how sweet the sound
That saved a wretch like me.
I once was lost, but now I'm found;
Was blind, but now I see.

Through many dangers, toils and snares
I have already come.
It's Grace that brought me safe thus far,
And grace will lead me home.

When we've been there a thousand years
Bright shining as the sun
We've no less days to sing God's praise
Then when we've first begun.

TRADITIONAL HYMN, 1760

The hypnotic call of death is beckoning, luring me with promises of peace for my haggard body. The assurance that I will no longer spit up blood, or worse, or continue to endure the excruciating coughs that consume my entire being, entices me. But I have conflict within. The powerful desire of my heart to stay with my husband and live life together is a strong one. The desire of my heart to always be there caring for my young and the fear that, if I am gone, the family will split apart keeps me fighting for each breath. I am now in my late forties and I do not know how much longer I will continue to win this battle against my flesh. In the time I have left I will write of my past, my times, my beliefs, and my testimony, that my influence will remain with my family when I have departed this world.

✎

Grandparents

No one could hope to grasp understanding of me if they do not understand the rich heritage of my origins. No matter how I feel about it, I now see how influenced I have been by my upbringing, my environment, and my extended family. Many of my mannerisms and the motives behind what I do come from those who lived before. I have every confidence I will have the same influence on my posterity. My heritage is rich and textured, full of hard work and faith. I would not want the good people of the past to be forgotten.

My Bostonian grandfather, Ebenezer Goddard, would insist on being first. As the story was told to me, he was a respected pillar of the community. He possessed a holy presence and, according to my mother, was much admired. While still in his youth, he was appointed sheriff of Middlesex County. He did a good job of it, too. He saw to it that "justice was done in the most strict manner."[1]

To characterize the man, words like charismatic, intelligent, and compassionate most fit him. He was also a gifted orator. If I had to sum up my grandfather's long sermons in one word, it would be "service." He practiced what he taught. The people who most seemed to seep into his heart despite his hard shell were the widows. Many women in the most desperate of situations sought his help. He never turned them away. In fact, he involved the whole family in helping these noble women as they courageously met the future. These ladies blessed the family in return with their humble examples. Long after my grandfather left this earth, ailing ladies embraced me with all tenderness and tears as they recounted their gratitude for my family.

According to Grandma Sybil, one of the greatest influences on Grandfather and herself was the dynamic minister John Wesley. Mr. Wesley was of the firm belief that the Sabbath should be observed with reverence and without silly, foolish variants that people use to excuse themselves from acting responsibly. Reading the Bible and taking our outline for life from the lessons found within those pages is another standard John Wesley adapted into his preaching to which our family adhered.

My mother's parents often sermonized from the Bible text. I do the same. Perhaps at times I display my grandfather's gift for the sermon. My grandmother Sybil would temper him, though, if he continued too long. "Ebb, it is supper time and we need to say grace." Or, "Your listeners are tired." Grandmother Sybil had a way of knowing how others felt and kindly pointed that out to her husband, for which we were all grateful.

My mother's side of the family has claim to a most unusual but truthful ghost story. Not only would the tale be told late at night to frighten the children, it was told to anchor in us the truth of God's power. During the times of witchcraft trials, when there was a heightened sense of evil, Grandfather Ebenezer was called on to champion the property of a widow. In this particular case, he opposed a powerful man who lived away from everyone in the village. There were rumors about the mysterious religious faith and unusual marriage of grandfather's opponent.

As Grandfather Ebenezer fought to help this widow defend her property, particular occurrences began to happen at his home. Papers that had been locked up in a desk disappeared, only to be found later in the dry well. Over and over again silt was found in the bottom of grandfather's fresh milk cans. The family supposed these happenings were the ill-deeds of their black slave. The slave was lectured, and when that did not solve the problem, he was beaten.

The strange events continued until one day Grandmother Sybil Goddard saw her day cap fall and at the same time her apron ripped itself in half. One part sailed up the chimney before she could do anything, but the other half she caught.

If that were not enough, she found the hearthfire covered by family books. Then the worst event of all, Grandmother Sybil watched the twin babies' clothing disappear up the stovepipe. She rushed to the babies who were then screaming and naked. Frantic, she tore up the house searching for who had done this and discovered no one. Whatever power was loose had broken all the boundaries by endangering the children and, of course, had to be stopped. Our family records tell how this was accomplished:

> They sent for many ministers, the most devout and holy men they could find. They got sixteen together at their house and they seemed to feel the importance of the occasion. They fasted two days and nights and the third day they spent in fervent prayer. There was one man among them that seemed more intent upon the subject than any other; he could not be denied; he pled with the Lord as a man would plead for his life, that he would break the power of the destroyer, that he would rebuke him and command him to leave the house and family forever. Towards night, on the third day when he was pouring out his soul with such fervor, and they were all in unity with him, in a moment there seemed to be a shock through the whole house, not of distress or sorrow, but of joy and assurance that there was a God in the heavens, whose ears could be penetrated with the cries of his children, and who was not slow to answer the prayers of those that put their trust in him. From that hour not a thing of the kind ever took place in their house or anywhere about them.[2]

This story had been the model in our family of the power of exercising our faith. I keep the tale deep within my heart and work to apply its lessons to my circumstances when I struggle with the frightening storms that press upon my family.

I cannot think of Grandfather Ebenezer without recalling this tale. He told me often, even though it shamed him, how he treated his slave. "Let that be an example of how jumping to hasty conclusions can cause problems, Nabby," he would say. "Do not do it." He would then shake his head, his thick silver hair barely moving. Then he grew silent as I sat on his lap and he rocked, his thoughts wandering back to another time.

I do not know why, but whenever he told this story, I listened. It was not only because Grandfather always commanded everyone's attention when he spoke, but there was an undercurrent in his tone that made me sad for him.

When I talked to my mother about how oppressive the story was, she would disagree. She thought it was a happy tale that proved Jacob's ladder was not broken, but that angels still descended and ascended it.[3]

Next I must write of my father's parents. In some ways both my grandfathers were a lot alike, in that Grandfather John Howe was also a respected religious man in his community of Hopkinton. Also, both men served in politics. Grandfather John's position was as the first town councilman. While Grandfather Ebenezer's focus was on service, especially regarding the needs of the widows, Grandfather John's specialty was the religious atmosphere of the town. Grandfather John believed that his town was in grave danger because the townspeople took the commandments of God too lightly. Grandfather John knew that proper instruction was vital in order to avoid certain destruction. Grandmother had dreams of warning which only fueled the fire within Grandfather. He decided to take action. With Grandmother's blessing and a farewell kiss, he traveled to Boston to obtain a pastor for the town. He had been instructed not to return home until he was successful in recruiting a religious leader. This task proved to be harder than expected, but after much persistence and patience, Samuel Barrett of the North Church agreed to come.

The religious tide was turbulent during that time, and my grandfather and Samuel Barrett rode it out with grit, determination, and a few compromises. One of those compromises was to allow communion for those who were not living worthily. My grandfather feared that if he did not lessen the standards, the church would dwindle. Reluctantly, he decided to focus on helping build others' conversions, to increase their faith instead of insisting that they live the highest standards. His compromise gave people another chance to straighten out their lives.

Grandfather John was also very different than Grandfather Ebenezer. Grandfather Ebenezer was boisterous and fluent with language. Grandfather John was more mild-mannered and patient.

Both of my grandfathers married complimentary wives. Grandfather Ebenezer married a feisty woman, who let him know when he pushed too far. She was unafraid to engage him in intellectual debates also. She loved the thrill of the spar. I enjoyed watching the two go at it. Grandmother Sybil was good. She would let Grandfather think that he had gotten the upper end of a conversation. She added some compliments to his points. Grandfather would boast, then she slipped in her reasons where he was faulty.

Grandmother Howe, on the other hand, was peaceful and avoided conflict. If a lively discussion broke out, she would slip away and feed the birds in the back woods. She rarely smiled or talked, but when she spoke, what she said was useful and insightful. Both women worked hard and rarely complained about their circumstances.

⤝⤞

Parents

Now I write about my parents, who also loved me and had a deep influence on my life. I was blessed in the parents I had. They were good to me and provided me with the necessities of life. I fear I deeply disappointed them, but as to that, I will speak more later. My mother, Susanna Goddard Howe, is full of energy, even to this day. I have, at times, wondered if perhaps she will outlive me; I think she will—she is stubborn enough to live forever.

Mother was born September 25, 1742, in Farmingham,

Middlesex, Massachusetts. She was a young bride of only nineteen years when she married my father on the twenty-third of April, 1761, in the close-by town of Hopkinton, Massachusetts.

If I had to name one quality that perfectly represents my mother, it would be her devotion to her religion. In my childhood, she was a Bible quoting parent with the uncanny ability to find the perfect verse to use in the way she wanted to correct the errors of our ways.

We learned the Bible well under her tutelage. An incident that exemplifies this happened after my brother had taken my favorite red ribbon, refusing to give it back. He declared, "Proverbs 16:18, pride goeth before the destruction, and an haughty spirit before a fall."

My response was less than Christian. My mother overheard me and hurried out into the yard, wiping her flour-covered hands on her apron. "Nabby, remember Proverbs 15:4. 'A wholesome tongue is a tree of life: but perverseness therein is a breach in the spirit.'"

"He will not give me my ribbon," I said, in an effort to explain that it was not me who was perverse.

"A soft answer turneth away wrath: but grievous words stir up anger. Proverbs 15:1," Mother said.

I thought back over my recent study and remembered a good passage that made me feel I could quote scripture, too. I shot out, "And a man's foe shall be they of his own household."

Mother could not withhold her pleased smile. "Very good," she said before resolving the conflict.

Until I became skilled at quoting scripture myself, hearing verse had irritated me. The advantage of time has turned my feeling from annoyance to one of gratitude. Mother knew the Bible to be the word of God, and that what could be found within those covers was the truth. I have adapted that concept into my own way of doing things, though we differ on several key points. I believe a person needs to be saved, which she also believes, but I also think that God requires more of us than just a desire to be saved. I believe our actions affect our position in heaven. She says that is an insult to our Savior and to the sacrifice He has made for us. In spite of our differing view points, I am grateful that she gave me the word of God as a way to determine truth.

Despite our differences, I am also full of thanks that my mother radiated her devotion to God in many ways. One way she did this was in the requests she has made of me as an adult. She often asks that I pray for her and for people in her extended family, that they might develop an interest in the Redeemer's kingdom.[4] She encouraged this herself through visiting and letter writing to our Christian friends, requesting that they pray with us and for the people who were lost. The state of other souls consumed her attention. Not only was she worried about her neighbors, but she showed extra concern for those members of our extended family who had not embraced religion.

If my mother's devotion to God is her foremost characteristic, the second would have to be her ability to make things last. She lets nothing go to waste. She received a silk dress as a wedding gift that she still wears. She owned that dress most of her life, and it is still in excellent condition. I often wonder how she has avoided getting stains on the dress. I have marveled about this dress to my children as I try to teach them the principles of care and thrift.

Not only does Mother take care of her clothing, but she enjoys the belongings she possesses. "Some things," she says, as she strokes her silk dress, "can last a lifetime, and it is up to us to see that they do." I tried to pass this skill down to my children. It has come in handy, since buying new clothes has been almost unheard of in our lives, and spending money on unnecessary items has not been a luxury we entertained.

Father passed away almost eight years ago, and the ache is still as intense as when I first heard the news. He was a good man, known to the world as Phinehas Howe. Born October 22, 1735, in Hopkinton, Middlesex, Massachusetts, he died September 19, 1807, in the same town. He was a well-looked upon man who liked to get involved in the town affairs. I remember watching him attend town meetings. I was so proud of him, knowing that he was involved in important business that affected everyone who lived in the community. He would talk about the events of the town during our meals, which helped cultivate my love of current events and history. One of the times I was proudest of him was when he was involved in the signing of different letters from the Hopkinton town fathers to the Continental Congress.

The Continental Congress was a legislative assembly during the Revolutionary War. At first the assembly worked to organize the colonials in protest of Great Britain's Intolerable Acts in 1774, but after that it continued to operate as a center for the national government.

Father often talked about the structure of the Continental Congress. He said the people who served there were making history. They were standing up to England and telling the King that we had the ability to govern ourselves. Father disliked having the king make rules when he was so far removed from the situation. He said that the disadvantage of long distance and the thirst for power allowed corruption and other misunderstandings to run rampant.

Father was not one to trust people who had more authority than he. Often he talked about keeping an eye on them and keeping them under control with checks and balances. He frequently commented on how dangerous it was for anyone to get too much power and authority. He would shake his head and say anyone who got too much authority could not seem to handle it; it ruined them. Each person needed to be careful of power. Father taught us that possessing pride and thinking you can handle everything yourself can lead to destruction. He did not care if the power came from the government or the church. Men in authority needed to be watched and held responsible for every choice they made.

Father not only taught us about governmental power, but he sent us to subscription school and to singing school, which was my favorite activity. He also supported his children's attendance at church socials, which we—my sisters, brothers, and I—enjoyed immensely. Most importantly, Father saw to it that we attended church and were taught the precepts of God. Each one of my brothers and sisters and

myself were christened at Christ's Church, an interesting choice considering the flurry of religious activity that was heating up the nation.

Chapter 2

They, looking back, all th'eastern side beheld
Of Paradise, so late their happy seat,
Waved over by that flaming brand; the gate
With dreadful faces thronged and fiery arms.
Some natural tears they dropped, but wiped them soon;
The world was all before them, where to choose
Their place of rest, and Providence their guide.
They, hand in hand, with wandering steps and slow,
Through Eden took their solitary way.
Paradise Lost, John Milton 1667

Childhood

Spring burst forth in Hopkinton, Massachusetts, when God sent me to grace this earth the third day of May in 1766. I was born to Phinehas Howe and Susanna Goddard at a time when a new country and a new way of life was emerging. My parents reflected often on those times and how proud they were of their budding nation. Thirteen colonies had not only been established, but they were booming. My mother loved the fact that America could boast of large cities, such as Philadelphia, which had over 34,000 people. The young nation had grown to over two and a half million people. Despite the population boom, my parents and their neighbors struggled from the effects of a recession caused by England taxing our colonies as it contended with France for land claims.

Problems increased for my family when the English decided they would levy a tax on us to pay for the wars. Without consulting the colonies, they imposed a bill on colonists to pay one-third of the expenses to keep 10,000 British troops stationed here to protect us. My father had harsh words to say about the soldiers whenever he explained to me what had happened. But I could tell he was more upset about the root cause of the events because his jaw would tighten and his eyes would get a far away appearance as he explained how the mother England turned on her own people and took away the very reason many fought in the wars. On October 7, 1763, England declared that no colonist could settle beyond the crest of the Appalachian Mountains—without even considering the fact that many families already lived beyond that point. What were those families supposed to do?—sacrifice all they had struggled to win and possess simply because King George III, who lived across the great ocean, decided to impose new borders one day?

The young nation's troubles with England did not stop there. King George III decided to tax important items such as playing cards, newspapers, and dice—even marriage licenses! Every legal document was to be taxed. Chafing under the additional burden, the colonists boycotted the English and their goods and laws. Despite the dissatisfaction, the everyday affairs of life had to be attended to and people were primarily worried about their crops of tobacco, corn, rice, indigo, and wheat.

〜

I was the third of what would be eleven children born to my parents. My kin, the Howes, were well-known in the community. A portion of my relatives lived in England. Others braved the perils of the Atlantic and sailed to America to carve out a new life. Some of my kinsmen had the honor and great opportunity to attend a new university called Harvard. My family was actively involved in the township as freemen, proprietors, selectmen, representatives, and Indian commissioners.

We had many successful people of substance in my family tree. They were able to enjoy a few of the finer things in life. A lot of us were inclined to the pursuit of learning. We often expressed this in our enjoyment of reading. The love of books was a contagious disease, of which I saw many of my relatives afflicted, myself included. My parents handed down that inclination to me and I tried my best to spread the passion of reading to my children. My family enjoyed the feel of leather bindings against their hands, the sound of the crisp pages turning, and the sight of the dark ink standing out against the white page. Mystery, knowledge, thoughts that could lead us closer to God were found within the magic of books. Some of my favorites were John Donne's "Holy Sonnets," Milton's *Paradise Lost*, John Bunyan's *Pilgrim's Progress*, Christopher Marlowe's "Dr. Faustus," George Herbert's poetry, and Shakespeare's sonnets.

Procuring books was difficult because we lived far away from the bigger cities, but my mother saw to it that I received reading material "to help aid me through the long winters," she said.

The influence of my family origins was clear, not only in the long tradition of learning but also in the hardy appearance of several of my children. John, Lorenzo, and Brigham looked much like the Howes: tall, strong, and sturdy. My oldest son, Joseph, took after his father, who was not as large in stature.

I stray from telling about my childhood. From the time I can remember, I was accustomed to listening to long discussions of complaint over Great Britain. Even at a young age and uninterested in politics, I knew that relations with England grew more hostile. This caused me little worry as I was too young to understand what was happening. To me at that time, Shrewbury, the New England town I lived in, felt safe. The community was hooked together in an endless stream of farms, like a comforting quilt. I have fond memories of growing up there. The nation, though, hit trouble by the time I reached the age of four.

My fellow countrymen were not pleased at paying the increased taxes for the assistance of the British soldiers. From the way I heard it, many of the colonists felt their father, the king, was trying to punish them for misbehavior. The soldiers paraded the streets of Boston as the result of colonial protests.

Despite the fact that taxes were increased, the soldiers did not feel they were being paid enough, and many of them took extra jobs to make ends meet. The soldiers did not mix well with the Bostonians; many disagreements were reported.

My mother especially liked to comment on these events by saying, "A house divided against itself shall not stand." Like fighting children, the soldiers and Bostonians clashed until their disagreements finally erupted on March 5, 1770. For years my mother used this as an example as to why we, her family, needed to unite our hearts with God. The story of how this conflict increased is said to have begun with several mischievous people throwing rocks and snowballs at the British soldiers outside the Customs Home. With bayonets fixed, twenty more soldiers came to their companions' aid. Their appearance had a rippling effect and soon the soldiers' opponents had grown to over a hundred boys and men, who joined in with insults, showering the soldiers with rocks, sticks, and whatever else they could find.

In panic, a soldier fired a shot point-blank into the crowd. Other shots fired off, and three colonists were killed on the spot. Two more colonists were mortally wounded and six others injured. One of the people who died was believed to be a runaway slave from Framingham, Massachusetts, named Crispus Attucks, a descendant of African and Indian ancestors.

Samuel Adams, the governor of Massachusetts, wrote of this incident in the papers, calling it a massacre. He urged his fellow colonists to stand up against such injustices. This incident served to get the British troops removed from Boston after Governor Thomas Hutchinson agreed the soldiers had to leave. The troops were moved to islands off the Boston harbor.

John Adams, who later became the second president of the United States, bravely came to the soldiers' aid and served as their lawyer in October, 1770. By December the jury had reached a decision. Captain Thomas Preston and six of his men were acquitted; two other soldiers were found guilty.

My parents argued about this event for years. My father did not see these events from a "house divided" perspective, but rather as fitting Isaiah's prophecy about "they which lead thee cause thee to err, and destroy the way of thy paths" (Isaiah 3:12). He believed that the Bostonians needed to stand up against the tyrants who were not allowing our country to have liberty. My father secretly told me about how he had traveled to Boston unable to keep away from all the commotion. If Mother ever found out that was the reason for his trip, he would have been headed for a talking to.

When I was eight, the Boston Tea Party occurred. I was old enough then to hear the gossip. My mind filled with visions of dumping tea into the sea and what it would be like to swim, spitting tea instead of water out of my mouth.

Although I was caught up in the cares of youth and unaware of most adult concerns, my father would not let me be ignorant of the political tension that flared with the British passage of new laws called the "Repressive Acts." The Boston Harbor was shut down, and this was all people discussed, mostly with deep resentment and tears. How were they going to live with their supplies of food, medicine, and other goods withheld?

The colonies responded quickly, gathering in Philadelphia on September 5, 1774, to establish the First Continental Congress and make a pact to defend themselves against their enemy, the British. The promise was soon to be counted on when the minutemen made their ride in April of 1775 to announce the British were coming. This was the true beginning of the war.

I was ten at that time. Many men in our town left to fight, and few came back. The conflict seemed to drag on forever. It was not until I was eighteen years old that we finally declared victory and were able to praise the Lord for our freedom that had been earned from eight hard years of fighting.

Despite the political unrest, Shrewbury had many activities such as sleigh parties, quilting bees, picnics, and one of my favorite things, religious revivals. I, unfortunately, was born just after one of my favorite revivalists, Jonathan Edwards, had died. I read his sermons many times, and imagined what it must have been like to have heard him cry with true emotion:

The God that holds you over the pit of hell, much as one holds a spider or some loathsome insect over the fire, abhors you, and is dreadfully provoked. His wrath towards you burns like fire; He looks upon you as worthy of nothing else but to be cast into the fire; He is of purer eyes than to bear to have you in

His sight; you are ten thousand times more abominable in His eyes than the most hateful venomous serpent is in ours.[5]

And then, after he had everyone shaking from just thinking about how awful our state would be, to hear him declare, "Therefore, let everyone that is out of Christ, now awake and fly from the wrath to come. The wrath of Almighty God is now undoubtedly hanging over a great part of this congregation: Let everyone fly out of Sodom:'Haste and escape for your lives, look not behind you, escape to the mountains, lest you be consumed.'"[6] This inspired me to keep my spiritual reawakening alive so I, too, could be saved.

As I write of Shrewbury, my childhood home, it still seems like my home. I feel I am only away on a visit. I treasure the friendly neighbors who knew me since I was a babe in my mother's arms, the lush trees I used to climb when I hid from doing my chores, and the church house we attended each Sabbath. All these elements shaped who I have become. I have felt like a visitor passing time in the other places I have lived, until I returned to my roots at Shrewbury. My, how Shrewbury has summoned my soul over the years, especially when I was called to endure harsh winters in Vermont.

Chapter 3

Shall I compare thee to a summer's day?
Thou art more lovely and more temperate.
Rough winds do shake the darling buds of May,
And summer's lease hath all too short a date.
Sometimes too hot the eye of heaven shines,
And often is his gold complexion dimmed;
And every fair from fair sometimes declines,
By chance or nature's changing course untrimmed.
But thy eternal summer shall not fade
Nor lose possession of that fair thou ow'st;
Nor shall Death brag thou wanderest in his shade,
When in eternal lines to time thou grow'st.
So long as men can breathe or eyes can see,
So long lives this, and this gives life to thee.
William Shakespeare, *Sonnet 18*

Husband

My husband is not what one would call an attractive man. Mother used to say he looked like a twig that was about to snap. My John may be wiry and small, but his personality and presence more than make up for that. He is a man of passion and conviction, and I would follow him anywhere. When he enters the room, he takes instant command of the place. Many people look to him with respect, and his power seemed to penetrate deep within me from the first. I found him impossible to resist.

My mother and father surely were not pleased when I made my decision to marry him. Upset with what I was going to do, Mother tried to talk me out of my decision several times. She eventually relented and said, "If John is who you choose, may God bless you both."

Father, on the other hand, never relented in his protest until the wedding was over. He worried that if John died I would be stranded with no inheritance or livelihood. Even if John did not die, his father was a drunk and a gambler, and it would only be a matter of time before John gave in to his family's tendencies and abandoned me like his father had done his mother. There was no reason for such suffering if I would but make a wiser decision in my choice of matrimony.

I tearfully protested. I knew in my soul that John would do nothing to bring me shame. Father shook his head and said, "It is a matter of time. What kind of marriage can you have with a man like that? He was raised by black slaves in the kitchen. You are a delightsome girl who could marry anyone. Do not settle for an orphan."

"Father, he is a good man. He loves God and puts Him first. The other fellows are not like that."

"He is pretending, Abigail. It is all an act."

Those words stayed with me, with John, with my parents. Mother and Father only saw his lowly position in life and the little chance that he would make anything of himself. I must admit, an orphan boy is a lowly position. When John was six, his father, a medical practitioner, was killed in an accident by a falling tree in Framingham.

My father-in-law, Joseph Young, had fought the French under General Johnson to take Crown Point, which was an important property of which to have control. At least that was how John explained it to our boys. He said, "Anyone who had charge of that spot was sitting pretty. The person in power would have control over trade with Canada from the Hudson Valley, since all the exchanging was done by water travel on Lake Champlain."

The French, with the Indians by their side, became ruthless. Joseph fought to save as many men as he could during that war along the Canadian border by Lake George and Lake Champlain. His nights and days were filled with the grim, thankless task of removing arrows and bullets from wounded soldiers. The matchlock bullets did nasty damage to the boys, ripping into them as though they were paper, leaving large gaping holes. The repair work was done in the midst of much bleeding and dying and men were in the worst kind of agony. Joseph Young transported as many of the wounded as he could to shelter and there performed surgery without the aid of medication and the proper equipment. Perhaps living through the horrors of war was the reason my dear husband's father drank—to forget, to be spared those images.

Perhaps this sadness was in part passed down to my John.

From the way John remembered, his father was mighty proud to have been part of the effort of driving the French back and winning the land for the British. Joseph told John that he would not be here in the Americas if they had not won that war, which, of course, was true.

War and killing—those things were not what life was about; that was Satan diverting our focus away from being saved. There were wars that did need to be fought, and if God required us to give up our brave men in the cause, no matter the personal pain we suffered, then it must be so.

After the war ended and my father-in-law's medical skills were no longer needed on the battlefront, he settled in Hopkinton, Massachusetts. While there, Joseph gained a reputation for success-fully treating cancer. In fact, through that reputation, he met my husband John's mother.

John Hayden was ill with cancer and Joseph was called in as his specialist. Unfortunately, he was unable to save John's life, but Betsy, John's daughter, did not seem to hold it against him. Instead, she married Joseph. As a result of that union, my husband, John, was born March 17, 1763, the third child of six.

My father-in-law was not a saint. He battled the spirits found in the bottle, which he never managed to overcome. He also fell into corruption with gambling, which cost him his reputation as well as his money. This greatly crippled his family. His debts con-tinued to mount. After he died, all of his collectors set after my poor mother-in-law.

John did not often speak about what had happened or about his father, for that matter, except for telling the children that he had been a war hero. Despite how little John spoke of his father, the toll of losing him was a burden that his mother could not shoulder. Within two years of her husband's passing, my mother-in-law was forced to sell the farm and the family's possessions.

At this point, the townspeople stepped in and bound out the children to positions around the area. My John, only six years of age, went with his younger brother, Joseph Jr., age four, to a Colonel Jones, who happened to be one of my father-in-law's friends. Colonel Jones was a stern man, but also one of the truly wealthy men in Hopkinton. He married into some of his money when he wed the former owner of the estate's daughter. With that union, he was able to obtain a gristmill.

It is unfortunate that wealth does not guarantee a person good character. The Colonel did not pay attention to things of God, and his wife was worse. From the way John told it, she despised him and showed it by indulging herself in beating him.

John could not withstand her attacks, and ran off to escape one of her more passionate beatings. Colonel Jones responded by telling John, "You dog, why did you run away?"

My husband kept quiet about his master's wife's beating, but Colonel Jones must have understood, because he took over the job of punishing my husband, which he did in the barn.

At age fifteen, John ran away again, this time to join the Continental Army in June of 1780. He served in the 4th Massachusetts

Brigade of Musketry for six months, marching from place to place. After his term was over, he went back to work for the Colonel.

John could not stay away from the army and joined the Massachusetts Militia on August 10, 1781. This time he served for three months, doing more marching about until he caught the dreadful Yellow Fever. In the army hospital at Peekshie he suffered the ravages of the disease: he had a high temperature, his tongue turned brown, and he vomited black bile.

John was never one to shy away from difficulty, and he certainly did not when he joined the army again for the third time in March of 1782. This service lasted only six weeks. Although the duration of this assignment was short, his responsibilities were different from those of the other two episodes. He was ordered to go to Rhode Island to repair Fat Butte.

After John served in the war, he reluctantly returned to Colonel Jones's place, but this time he refused to work without a salary. However, Colonel Jones found a way to profit from John's work in the military. He took John's discharge papers and turned them in as payment on his own taxes.

Despite this annoyance and many others that resulted from being under Colonel Jones's rule, John was indebted to the Colonel for allowing him to work and for helping John survive until he reached manhood. Colonel Jones taught John many valuable skills which we have used all our married life, such as the care of the farm. I strongly believe that working with the land from early morning to dusk awakened something in my husband's soul. He fell deeply in love with the land, the smells, the dirt, the landscape. That love has always been an important part of John.

John worked for wages and then, soon after laboring on his own, he started to court me. He often told me he found it impossible to resist my light yellow hair, always curled in ringlets, and my eyes that were paler than the blue of the sky on a rainy day. He followed the proper way to court me, but I must admit I hesitated at first. He was not the most handsome of my suitors; nor the most well situated. Actually, as I thought about it, his place in the world was the worst I knew. But he did love God, and I found that devotion mighty attractive.

At last John was released from his apprenticeship when he arrived at the ripe old age of twenty-one in the spring of 1784. Our courtship danced to an end and our life together as a married couple started on October 31, 1785, at the Congregationalist Church. Pastor Elijah Fitch joined us in Hopkinton, Middlesex County, Massachusetts. I was twenty years old and John was twenty-two.

Through the courtship and our early marriage, politics integrated into our conversations, thoughts, and minds. The nasty Independence war against the English had been fought and won. We were free—free to pursue any life we wanted. Opportunities opened to us as long as we tried hard enough.

However, the effects of war were apparent everywhere. Widows struggled to eat, to live. Parents would burst into tears at church meetings as they stared out the window, knowing their son would never come bounding over the hill again. Oh, the heartache! The sisters talked about their brothers in soft, respectful voices, telling young friends who complained about some annoying brother that they would give anything to have their annoying brother alive again.

The destruction affected John, too. He frequently offered prayers of gratitude to the Great I Am, telling Him to please tell those boys that gave the ultimate sacrifice a big "thank-you" from him.

When John had time and was around other men, he would engage in lively discussions about the state of the country. John wanted the states to remain united. There was strength in unity. Winning the war against England did not offer a guarantee that there would not be additional problems. Many others held that each state should have its own independence and not be told what to do by the other states. John could appreciate this point of view, but when he participated in those discussions, I watched him stubbornly sticking to his opinion. He reminded me of a lion with his fierce determination—unrelenting and courageous as he clung to his values.

After the war, the people in town felt strongly about having hierarchical control hanging over them. Freedom to live their lives as they chose was precious to them. Hopkinton, like other small towns in the country, was hit hard by war debts. The citizens did not like the great expense it took to run the state, and there was much complaint. They also did not appreciate that the General Court was in Boston, that lawyer fees were so expensive, and that administrators' salaries were so heavy. Nor did the citizens approve of the court using large numbers of people to run the system.

These were some of the vital issues to be considered by those trying to form a new nation.

One of John's favorite politicians, whom he often quoted, was
John Adams, who had quite a reputation for his gift of speech. It
was as if everything he spoke was spun into golden threads for the
listeners' ears. My John kept up with Adam's doings.

When we were first married, John Adams, Benjamin Franklin,
and Thomas Jefferson took a trip across the sea to forge relations with
the European nations and to establish commercial trade. This would
be crucial for our newly formed nation's survival. My husband commented about these men and their activities constantly.

As I think back on those times and the way John was, I believe
if he would have been in different circumstances, if we had not had
our first child so early, and if we had more money, he would have
gone into politics himself. Throughout our life together, John was
friendly to everyone and was very well liked. Our neighbors had
respect for him. His reputation was one of dealing justly with all
with whom he came in contact. That reputation was well earned.
He would have done well in government. People liked John, and he
had excellent ideas.

John was also the hardest worker I have ever known. When it
came to work, he possessed the strength of an ox. He would start
before the sun came up and continue working long after it set,
unrelenting in his efforts to meet Mother Nature's deadline. His
work ethic gained him a reputation. He was known as "the best
mower in the section where he lived."[7]

Thus, despite his lack, John reigned as king in my heart. This truly was what kept me stable enough to endure the tremendous obstacles that would come to us in our lives together.

Chapter 4

When, in disgrace with fortune and men's eyes,
I all alone beweep my outcast state,
And trouble deaf heaven with my bootless cries,
And look upon myself and curse my fate,
Wishing me like to one more rich in hope,
Featured like him, like him with friends possessed.
Desiring this man's art and that man's scope.
With what I most enjoy contented least;
Yet in these thoughts myself almost despising,
Haply I think on thee, and then my state,
Like to the lark at break of day arising
From sullen earth, sings hymns at heaven's gate;
For thy sweet love remembered such wealth brings
That then I scorn to change my state with kings.
William Shakespeare, _Sonnet 29_

Hopkinton

John and I started our life together in Hopkinton, the same town where we met. The town was mid-sized compared to the others surrounding it. Not everyone knew everyone else, but if we did not personally know them, we had heard of them. It seemed as though the entire town was one huge family, as almost everyone was related either by bloodline or through marriage. And though this created some challenges, it also engendered a forgiving attitude in overcoming disagreements and difficulties.

While at Hopkinton, John worked hard to keep us fed and clothed. He put in lengthy days, which he did not seem to mind—but I did, at times. I was a young bride and longed for him to be by my side as much as possible. Although I would dream of us spending endless days laughing, hugging, and spending time together, drinking in each other's souls, the reality of life quickly swept that sweet, unrealistic vision away.

Ten months after we were married, I gave birth to my first child, Nancy, on August 6, 1786. I remember when the midwife first held her up before my eyes. I was overwhelmed with awe and reverence that I had actually given birth to a living, breathing human being. What a weighty responsibility. She was a beautiful baby with long slender fingers and a sprinkling of light brown hair. She was the perfect child to start me off in the experience of motherhood. At first I had much fear of breaking her or of hurting her in some other way. I hovered over Nancy to make sure she was breathing and that all else was all right. I spent many nights counting the seconds between her breaths. My fear did fade, but her crying and dislike of nursing remained. Often Nancy wrinkled up her nose and kicked her feet straight up making her legs stiff. John and I would joke that she was wrestling with Jacob's angel again.

Our second daughter, Fanny, came along on November 8, 1787, so that my two oldest were only fifteen months apart. The girls became close friends; of course, they had spats, but whenever such outbreaks occurred, I had both of them sink to their knees to ask forgiveness from their Maker, and peace was restored once again.

✺

Durham

One never knows how good her situation is until it is changed. This was certainly true for me. I had the many struggles of a young wife and mother, being tired, often worn-out, anxious about raising my children well, and longing for more time with my husband, dreaming of more peace and well-being between us. Those years seem to be a blur comprised of John and I laboring with the children and the farm, confronting all the challenges of starting a new family. I am shamed to admit that in the midst of this I took for granted some of my greatest blessings.

In 1789 my husband announced we were moving from Hopkinton. Pain clutched my heart at the prospect of leaving my parents, friends, and town. I had not realized before what a blessing having my parents close by had been. Their presence brought reassurance that, although I was living independently, the option to go to them in desperate circumstances existed, and everything would be fine. This unappreciated security was being removed.

John had grown tired of the place and wanted to move on and see if another town would offer our family a better existence. He often talked about providing me with everything that I had enjoyed when I lived with my family. I wished he did not worry about that. It did not matter if we were poor for the rest of our lives as long as I could stand by his side and serve God.

John had his heart set on a place called Durham in Greene County, New York, on the eastern side of the Catskills, and a little south of Albany. Many other Revolutionary War veterans had moved there, too. But this place held sadness for John. His older brother, William, had died there only a few years earlier after he was trampled by a horse. Despite this, John was determined to work his way there.

I was deeply saddened to exchange life in Hopkinton for the hard frontier existence, with few neighbors nearby, but felt that I must in order to support my husband. It was important for him to do what he believed was required for him to care for his family.

Once at Durham, John set his farming skills to use. He cleared the land and farmed the soil. He would come in during mealtime and a sense of satisfaction and accomplishment could be felt. Not only did we harvest crops and food for our family, but in September of 1789 we also welcomed a third baby girl into our family, who I named Rhoda, after my beloved sister.

Girls have a way of stirring a man's heart; John was very tender with his string of daughters. But despite his happiness, I knew John yearned for a boy-a son to follow in his steps, to carry on his name.

He did say several times when I was pregnant and I would suck in my breath from a powerful kick, "Was there a bit of extra strength to that kick, Nabby?" John desperately wanted to have that father-son relationship, which he was cheated of when his own father's life was cut short.

It was in Durham that John and I joined the Methodist church. There were circuit riders who came to visit us at our cabin. They talked about the good Lord, which we are always willing to discuss. The Methodist riders performed baptisms, funerals, and held revivals. They took care of those of us who lived out where neighbors were few and far between. I was impressed with their dedication to us. The Methodist riders did not take religion for granted. It meant something to them and they were willing to make sacrifices to prove it. Besides, they did not preach foolish concepts, such as a person relying on the strength of a single experience. No, the Methodists had more sound principles. They believed, as John and I did, that true conversion comes from within you, that your whole being must be dedicated to the Lord. A person could tell if he were truly dedicated to the Lord not by what he said or what he wanted, but by what he did. Did his or her deeds have the spirit of God in them?

While we stayed in Durham, I experienced the beginnings of a trial that would plague me for the rest of my life. Week after week of backbreaking work clearing the land wore me down and I grew ill. At first I felt a slight cough developing, but I did not think anything

of it and kept at my work. The cough was only there in the morn-
ings when I rose out of bed. Slowly, over time, the cough grew worse.
I treated my fatigue and cough with different herbs and natural
remedies, which greatly aided my comfort, but had no power over
the ravages of the disease. Some days I felt almost normal, and could
work as hard as I had in the past. Other days I would be too weak
and ill to do much at all. The illness settled in my lungs and chest, and
I grew more and more fatigued as though there were a leak near my
heart draining my strength and my will to fight. My fatigue and lack
of ability to keep the housework done laid a burden upon the other
members of my family. My children and my husband made efforts to
keep our home clean and the household running smoothly, but they
lacked the skills. Early on when I so much wanted to be helping, I felt
frustrated with inferior work. Later I learned to submit myself to
God's will and not focus on what was wrong, but on what was right.
When I did that, I was able to bask in gratitude for my family's will-
ingness to pitch in and for what they did do. This experience of learning to not demand that everything be perfect, but accept the best out
of others, was humbling for me.

This battle against what I finally accepted as the dreaded consumption continued for years. There were times when I thought I
was healed. Then I was in a long winter, had little food, and the
cough returned. As I write, I am still plagued with this illness, but
with no hope that the cough will go away. But I am straying from
the story. I want to tell everything while I have the chance.

⤜⤐

Hopkinton, Once More

My heart filled with joy when John announced we would be moving back to Hopkinton. I could not help constantly thinking about the glorious times I would have renewing old friendships and seeing people who had remained so precious to my heart.

It was a reluctant return for John; to him it was defeat. But I was glad to be with my family. My parents were much pleased about the move. They had pleaded constantly for us to return. Perhaps, to please them, to convince my parents that he was not just an orphan boy, John agreed to come back. It was true that John was a conscientious man who wanted to make me happy. Although he never said it, I knew he felt guilty that he had taken me from my parents and the comfortable life I lived to a wild, hard existence on the frontier. Then, with my health taking a turn for the worst, his guilt and fear deepened, I am sure.

It grieved me to see John feel that way. He came from a terrible childhood, and suffered grievances that I can only guess at. I have watched his heroic efforts to rise above the mistreatment. He struggles with his temper, but continues to pick himself up when he has fallen and try again. I admire him for that.

I believe another reason for the move back to town was that John finally admitted to himself that the land in Durham was not good. It was impossible to clear a forest. He would work night and day and be lucky for the few plants that pushed through the rocky soil. The work was challenging and the rewards rare.

John often talked of his conviction that he would, given enough time, provide a plentiful life for his family.

The day finally came when our wagon rolled into Hopkinton, and many people gathered to welcome us. So many familiar faces circled about that I felt we were on holiday. When I saw my mother though, I shrank back when I saw how wrinkled and frail she had become. Age had been changing her, and the realization of this changed me.

When we embraced, unexpectant tears came. I held on tightly to her as though I would lose her forever if I let go. After all my years of independence, I still needed her. Inside I was still that little girl looking to my mother to alleviate the woes and pains of life.

>~~~

In 1790, we established our home on Sadler's Hill. We arrived in town with three children in tow, but that number quickly increased. Soon John got his boy, who we named John. Though this was a high point to finally give birth to a boy, I remember soon after his birth that I sank into a dark sadness. My John left every morning before light to toil in the muddy soil, preparing the land for seed. Later in the week there was to be a barn raising that John and the others would be attending. I longed to go, too, for there were few times I had the chance to be with neighbors and enjoy other women's company.

Instead of going to the barn-raising or even tending the new baby, I laid in bed, a few tears escaping. I was too ill to rise and rock the baby. Besides, my coughing and choking seemed to frighten the child. Fanny attended to John Jr., hushing his whimpers as Nancy prepared the meal. This was not the life I had anticipated. I remember drifting off with the pain and not awakening until late that evening. The fire had burnt down to a low orange. John slept next to me, looking like a large mound of lumpy potatoes. A cough gripped me which I tried to hold back, not wanting to disturb the family.

When the coughing spell died down, thoughts of my childhood came like soft music. I remembered myself dancing through the hills collecting flowers, or putting my whole heart into the songs I sang for the church choir. These were sweet thoughts of a life which I would live no more.

I had traded the town life, friends, socials, and new dresses for John and my children. Although John had a roughness about him, he had ambition to rise from it. The children, although taxing at times, had sweet, loving natures. As I reflected on my blessings I felt a peace engulf me, lifting me from the dark shadows that had been pressing down on me earlier. *We are all in God's hands*, I thought as I drifted to sleep.

Despite my illness, children continued to come. Nabby was born on April 23, 1793, Susannah on June 17, 1795, Joseph on April 7, 1797, and Phinehas Howe on February 16, 1799.

Events of the nation kept many in Hopkinton speculating on what would become of our newly-formed country. In April 1789, George Washington became the new president of the free and independent United States. Our family wished we could break away from our farm responsibilities to see him, but this would not be possible. Therefore we resolved ourselves to reading the newspapers, which reported parades and crowds gathered everywhere our new president visited. My John said that Washington was not much of a politician as far as playing the negotiating games but, despite that, President Washington did a fine job, and possessed the wisdom to surround himself with the best and most honorable of men. For example, John Adams became Vice President; Alexander Hamilton, Treasurer; Thomas Jefferson, Secretary of State; Henry Knox, Secretary of War; and Edmund Randolph, Attorney General.

We often prayed for these men in the heavy responsibilities they faced. These great thinkers must have played their part in keeping us out of the French Revolutionary War brooding in Europe. As the conflict overseas spread, our apprehension increased that the Bible revelations of the end of times were unfolding. Mounting pressure fell upon our young nation to become involved. Britain often engaged in impressment runs, stopping our ships and forcing our sailors to serve in their navy. The French were no better, attacking our ships heading for England. I was relieved that we did not become involved, fearing my husband, brothers, and uncles would have to fight. My husband wanted to stand up against the injustices suffered by the French people, as we had been helped so recently in our cause.

Our different perceptions led to many interesting conversations.

By March 1790, the first census was completed, revealing that our new nation had a population of 3,929,625, as my mother was pleased to report. Philadelphia was now the largest city, with New York following close behind.

The country suffered a great loss when eighty-four-year-old Benjamin Franklin died on April 17, 1790. I was distraught at the news. I reflected on what he had done for our country, all of which my family now benefited from. I felt as though I had lost someone close to me although I had never met the man. I joined the country in mourning. The sadness lifted somewhat with the news that Rhode Island had finally endorsed the Constitution at the end of May. With the Constitution firmly in place, Congress made plans for the location of the home of our national capital. The newspapers reported their decision to build it on a site along the Potomac River.

Along with our family making moves, Congress did, too. They relocated from New York to Philadelphia. I suppose the congressional wives hated moving from one place to another, knowing they would have to pick up and leave again. I hated moving, too, but at least I did not know I would be doing it again.

Two more states joined our country; Vermont, in 1791, and Kentucky, in 1792. These additions were welcomed, giving us the sense that our nation was growing and becoming stronger, as was my family.

While I settled fights between brother and sister at home, a feud developed on the political front between Thomas Jefferson and

Alexander Hamilton. Both men viewed politics differently. They did their fighting in the newspapers. Jefferson's views were published in the *National Gazette* and Hamilton's in the *Gazette of the United States*. These articles spawned debates throughout our small town, which my husband John loved to engage in, and to which I would listen whenever my labors and children would allow.

Another big event that caused talk was the Whiskey Rebellion. Congress put a tax on distilled spirits—which should have been even higher, if you ask me. The people who participated in drinking the evil substances grew angry that they could not sin as easily. In 1794 they formed a militia, the *Mingo Creek Society*. One day an inspector, John Neville, was doing his job and the Mingo Creek militia marched on him. One of Mr. Neville's slaves shot and killed him, igniting an open rebellion. The problem was only resolved when George Washington marched to the area with 13,000 men to stop the rebels.

While that part of the country fought, my parents gave me a book written by a woman named Mary Wollstonecraft, who wrote *A Vindication of the Rights of Women*. I spent the cold nights after Bible reading poring over her words:

After considering the historic page, and viewing the living world with anxious solicitude, the most melancholy emotions of sorrowful indignation have depressed my spirits, and I have sighed when obliged to confess, that either nature has made a great difference between man and man, or that the civilization which has hitherto taken place in the worlds have been very partial. I have turned over various books written on the subject of education, and patiently observed the conduct of parents and the management of schools; but what has been the result?—a profound conviction that the neglected education of my fellow-creatures is the grand source of misery I deplore; and that women, in particular, are rendered weak and wretched by a variety of concurring causes…men have been more anxious to make them alluring mistresses than affectionate wives and rational mothers…when they ought to cherish a nobler ambition, and by their abilities and virtues exact respect.

As I think about my daughters and the places in society they may acquire, there is one truth I want them to take and make their own. Man might be the landowner, voters, and government leaders, but all these positions lack the power the woman can claim as her own. The man might lead nations, but it is the woman and her influence that makes that man. Her touch, her soft spoken words can subtly change minds and hearts. The effectiveness of this power lies in subtlety. A woman who is wise uses her tempering influence for good. In order for a woman to best exercise her influence she must acquire education, as Mary Wollstonecraft advocated.

Our children rarely attended regular schools, for their help was much needed on the farm. Despite this I desired them to have the gift of reading. I used any free time I could snatch to gather them around and teach them to read, write, and do sums. Most often this would be done in the evenings. I was able to do a good amount of this teaching from my bed and between my coughing fits, but as it grew increasingly more difficult, our heaven-sent older children took over much of this task. Oh, how I wished I had the energy to teach the children as I wanted to. But I pressed on, trying to do what my frail body allowed me, even though I grew weaker. I especially liked to have Nancy read to me. It helped take my mind away from the excruciating pain. Other times I needed it quiet. I would go deep within myself and pray to Father above for mercy.

When I did do schooling, I would gather the children around the warming fire and set to work. We started with prayer. For the most part our children were eager learners, although sleep often fell on them. That was our greatest struggle. I used the Bible as our text. What greater book to learn from?

Not only did we work on education, but I spent time teaching them proper hymns, especially when we toiled at our chores. I loved to hear our children's sweet voices singing praises to the Lord. My children were gifted in carrying notes. We often made our way through the day singing every hymn I could recall.

When I was not teaching my children, reading from the Bible, or singing hymns, we gathered together and listened to my John tell his lively stories of the vast experiences he had serving in the war and fighting for our liberation. He also told the children great tales about working on Colonel Jones's plantation. Oh, how the children loved hearing them. They begged him to repeat the stories again and again. I wondered though if those stories were true and how much they were exaggerated over the many tellings. But John's deep voice stroked the air with a calming effect. As I grew more and more ill, I was confined to bed listening to the sound of his voice roaring like a lion. I often closed my eyes and let the words drift away as the rhythm of his voice and the rhythm of the children's laughter and delight almost took me away from the pain.

John was an excellent storyteller and I loved this about him. It helped bring the family close together. Every one of our children enjoyed hearing his deep voice fall into a story. As our older children brought children into the world, they made a habit of gathering their little ones onto their knees to begin the tale for the evening. What a satisfying way for the family to learn their history and for us to enjoy time together. I hope this tradition never ceases in our family.

Honoring God through acceptable forms of worship was of utmost importance to John and me. The frontier did not always offer many exterior opportunities. When we could not find a church, we worshipped at home. When we could find a church, we leaned toward the Methodists. Ever since our experiences in Hopkinton, Massachusetts, we had an extra liking for them. The members were God-fearing, simple people who struggled like we did.

Unfortunately, over time the Methodist church allowed Congregationalist thoughts to intrude on their beliefs. It was nonsense to me that the church weaned itself away from the fundamentalist principles, like baptism by immersion and faith by healing. I knew from experience that healing was real.

Other churches surrounding us were the Sadducees and Pharisees of our day, the Congregationalist Church with preachers who received their big degrees at Harvard and Yale.

I thought we were going to live in Hopkinton for the rest of our lives, but the moving fever affected our neighbors and eventually the desire to leave seeped into John. It was all he could think or talk about, moving west and getting blessed with improved living conditions, more crops, a better life. We were, I have to admit, struggling as we lived in Hopkinton, although I loved the place. More than once we toiled to find food, and at times it simply was not possible.

I decided I would rather see my children well fed than growing up in the town I loved. I gave my support to picking up our belongings and traveling to where John believed God directed. Besides, if only half of what people said about the bounty of the soil in New York was true, we would have a much-improved life.

We also had an opportunity offered to us because John was a Revolutionary soldier. Tracts of land were reserved as homesteads for the men who served so bravely for our country. We saw an advertisement by Phelps and Gorham, listing all the advantages of going west and beginning anew. It looked like a promising opportunity, but for some reason John did not have a good feeling about a move to New York.

As the nation was getting a new president, John Adams, my John felt we as a family needed to go through a change also. Rejecting the idea of a move to New York, he decided on moving to Whitingham, Vermont. Why? I never was quite sure. He said that was where we were going. Once he made up his mind, there was nothing that could be done except to fall into step.

Chapter 5

The Frost performs its secret ministry
Unhelped by any wind. The owlet's cry
Came loud-and hark, again! loud as before.
The inmates of my cottage, all at rest,
Have left me to that solitude, which suits
Abstruser musings: save that at my side
My cradled infant slumbers peacefully.
'Tis calm indeed! So calm, that it disturbs
And vexes meditation with its strange
And extreme silentness. Sea, hill, and wood,
This populous village! Stream and hill, and wood,
With all the numberless goings-on of life,
Inaudible as dreams! The thin blue flame
Lies on my low-burnt fire, and quivers not;
Only that film, which fluttered on the grate,
Still flutters there, the sole unquiet thing.
Methinks its motion in this hush of nature
Gives it dim sympathies with me who live,
Making it a companionable form,
Whose puny flaps and freaks the idling Spirit

By its own moods interprets, everywhere
Echo or mirror seeking of itself,
And makes a toy of Thought.
                    Samuel Taylor Coleridge, *Frost at Midnight*,
                    February, 1798

Whitingham

*W*e spent most of our time eeking out an existence in the
breath-taking, unforgiving land of southern Vermont. Our
children were raised to labor exhausting hours, first working as ten-
ants on overworked land, then cultivating new land and building
homes in which to dwell.

The unrelenting pressure of providing for the family weighed
heavily on John. This is perhaps what drove him to search constantly
for better land conditions. So when John took an extra liking to
the land in Whitingham, although I was saddened by the reality of
moving again, it came as no surprise for me or the children. John
Jr. tried many times, while working along side his father in the fields,
to convince John that we could remain. My husband grunted about
focusing on the work at hand.

My husband kept his eagle eye on the land until 1797. There was
a disagreement over property on which the landlord had obtained a
patent before the Revolutionary War. Years before, folks had wan-
dered onto that corner of Vermont and settled. Being honest folks,

we waited for years, making sure the land was open and no one would claim we stole it. No one heard a thing about the previous landlord for years, so finally, John talked me into settling with the children in tow.

In November of 1800, John purchased fifty acres in Lot 21 of "Fitches Land Grant" in the village of Whitingham, from his sister's husband. John paid fifty dollars, which we thought was a good price. Whitingham lay along the Deerfield River a few miles north of the Massachusetts border.

After we offered many prayers of thanks to our Maker, we made plans for our new dwelling. The first decision we were called upon to make was what time of year to move. After much deliberation, we chose to leave in January. Most of the roads would be impossible to travel through in spring and fall due to mud which caused the wagons to sink into ruts so deep the bed of the wagon would rest on the surface of the ground. In summer, the dryness of the roads brought the problem of dust. In winter, although bitter cold, the bobsled wagons could slide easily over the frozen ground.[8] Traveling in January, our journey was far from easy, although we did avoid the troubles with dust and mud. The trip was over 100 miles, which took about ten days. It being winter in Vermont, we were greeted by heavy snowstorms and their side effects. To protect our young children, my older girls wrapped the little ones tight in blankets, holding them fast, to shield them from the biting cold.

The move required us to use two horse-pulled bobsleds, which John and the boys built by mounting wagon boxes onto runners. We used one of the bobsleds for the children and myself. The other bob-sled carried our belongings.

Joseph, three, would often struggle out of thirteen-year-old Fanny's arms, not wanting to miss any of the experience. He would laugh as cheerfully as a bubbling spring when the bobsled swooped down a hill, bouncing through the high drifts. When going uphill, he would hold his face square into the cold snappy wind.

Fanny, always a skittish child, would meanwhile be ducking behind her younger brother crying out, "Mother, Joseph will not sit."

The last days were long and hard. Joseph's earlier delight faded into tears. Fanny gathered him in blankets and sat on top of our belongings in the back of the bobsled. She told stories of princes and princesses, knights, castles, and gloriously warm summer days. Joseph would calm to sniffles as the rest of us tried to overhear the tale above the intense howl of the wind that blew in from Canada.

The children's complaints ceased as the temperatures dropped below zero. The cold penetrated deep in our bones. I constantly warned the children to wiggle their hands and feet to avoid frostbite. The cold continued to press upon us as the pelting of freezing rain pounded our belongings and caused the bobsled to slide wildly. At these times, my boys gave nervous laughs and the girls screamed high-pitched wails, all but Fanny. She would wait until the sliding stopped, then she immediately continued her story.

A few hours later, the temperature would take a dramatic change and warm up. But the warmth and the pleasure derived from it were halted as the sky opened up and unleashed buckets of rain.

If it had not been so miserable, this weather would have been an exquisite sight to behold, because whatever stood in the way of the freezing rain had glittering sheets of ice covering it.

After their first experience with the ice rain, the second one caused Nancy, fourteen, and John, Jr., nine, to tell jokes and call each other yellow bellies. The younger girls' nerves were ragged. Fanny stopped with her stories and gripped her blanket tightly. Nabby, seven, and Suannah, five, cried along with the younger children as John yelled at them, "Stop your nonsense. It is not going to help." Then he took charge of the panic.

He surveyed our conditions and noted that the moment the rain touched anything it transformed into ice.

John ordered Rhoda, eleven, to tend to the stock and settle their nerves.

"I will go," I protested.

"Not in your condition," John said.

"But—"

"Nabby, I will not have you lose this baby. Settle the younger children. We will see to the rest." There was nothing I could do but obey and pray until we had secured shelter.

John's reference to my unborn child who I had only recently felt moving set me off to my worries. Since I had contracted consumption, each time I saw the signs of another child I wondered if I would live to raise it. What would happen to my child if I died? Would John be able to cope? The idea of leaving my children motherless sinks me into a silent foreboding.

My prayers were also for our ice-encrusted animals, who had no protection from the weather. I prayed that the good Lord would make their fur coats thick to temper their sufferings.

Not only did the animals struggle, but the mighty branches of the oaks and maples grew weak under the pressure of the frozen rain. Sometimes the layer of ice was a full half inch thick. We could hear the sound of the periodic collapse of huge limbs roaring over the hills. Loud cracks and breaks of shifting ice echoed through the Green Mountain area across the frozen ponds.

As the days wore on and the snow deepened, our energy and zest for the move waned. It did not help that the older children complained of being stuck with the younger ones. "She will not listen to me" and, "He will not stop crying" were frequent protests. All we could do was press on, and thank the Lord that He had preserved us in our journey thus far.

The Lord truly extended His hand to us to carry us safely to another great opportunity. I reminded the children of the restless bunch of Israelites who traveled with Moses and how that mighty prophet had to patiently endure the ungrateful chosen people who moaned about their plight for forty years. Finally a hush would fall on the children. I was not sure if it was because they understood their error or that John had come back to camp and whacked a few of them for their fretting, and the others did not want to draw his attention.

Before John, myself, and our children left Whitingham, my parents wrote a letter requesting that Rhoda stay with them. My first impulse was to clutch Rhoda to my chest and say, "No."

I told John about the letter as he chopped wood. He swung the ax ruthlessly before stopping and asking, "Do you want her to go?"

We engaged in much talk about the subject over the next few weeks. My heart was torn. Rhoda was the delight of the family, a peace maker who avoided conflict with anyone. She had a gift of easing the contention that arose by soothing hurt feelings through soft touches and gentle words. Her manner even had a calming affect on John when his anger flared.

When pain gripped me, twisting me in agony, Rhoda was the one who noticed and would quietly sit by my side and stroke my hands and hair. This eased my suffering. For this reason and many more, parting with Rhoda seemed unthinkable, except for the fact that my parents were aging and needed assistance. I could not move far from my parents and abandon them. John said nothing when I spoke to him of what I thought should be done. He gave a curt nod, as though he was unaffected by this decision, but his clouded eyes seemed to be storming in pain.

I whispered to him the positives of letting Rhoda go. Rhoda would be staying in a home much more comfortable than what we could at present provide. She would, through association with my parents, have status in the community.

"You are telling me that if Rhoda goes she will have the life you left when you married me."

I brushed at my apron as though I was straightening it.

John was not one to deny our daughter Rhoda a chance at better privileges. We gave our consent to let our daughter go. Little did we know how much this decision would deeply affect us.

Finally we made the move to Whitingham. We were grateful to find neighbors who graciously greeted our family, and welcomed us into their homes until we could provide adequate shelter for ourselves. At first, our neighbors consisted of the Wheelers, Fullers, Faulkners, and Sayers. Good folk. It would have been awfully lonesome without them. After John and the boys cut down enough trees for a log-raising, all the neighbors turned out. I did enjoy log-raising events, an excuse for long put-off, but much needed visiting among the ladies.

The land was filled with a multitude of rocks, ravines, and ridges. But I felt I was admiring an artful masterpiece as I looked down the ravines onto the thousands of trees below. Sometimes I stopped my work to catch my breath and gaze over the green rolling hills and the full-grown fir, maple, and birch trees which composed the forest. I thanked Father above for such beauty. The sky in Vermont often turned deep blue with the clouds so white I could almost see the angels sitting on them watching me and my family as we struggled to live a proper life, dedicated to the Lord, grateful for His goodness in preserving us.

Another thing that gave me much satisfaction was the demanding work of "sugaring off." Collecting the sap from the enormous maple trees on our lot was satisfying for my sweet tooth. My children must have been a lot like me, because they seemed much happier when late March came around and the sap basins were filled. A pleasure the children and I enjoyed when John was busy elsewhere was to take the recently collected maple syrup and pour some onto clean snow. The syrup and the snow mingled to create a delicious frozen sugary treat. The children never tired of eating this dessert. I must admit, neither did I.

In Vermont, we found the Reformed Methodist church, where people were concerned about following the Bible more strictly, which was the way it should be. God's word should not be changed or varied. Finding a church that supported God's way held high value for us.

The reminders to go to church and not violate the Sabbath were significant. Of course, there could never be too much preaching against the evils of liquors, or how vital maintaining one's virtue was. The church taught the importance of family prayer, which in our house was offered almost without fail; we needed as much guidance as possible.

Another thing my children were taught when we attended the meetings was the importance of honesty in all avenues of life, and especially in business transactions. They were taught that even when starving or going without could make it tempting to cheat your neighbor, if any dishonesty was given into, it was cheating the Lord.

>⫶⟋⟍

June 1, 1801 was a day of heat, sun, and intense pain. Another child had been born to our family. The child was a boy with chunky cheeks, otherwise thin and healthy. But I was too weak and ill to hold him and lovingly care for him as I desired.

Reports came to me a day later that Fanny had taken up the infant, his new skin covered in hair so light it reminded me of peach fluff. Fanny hovered over the child, answering his cries for food and sustenance both day and night, forging a bond that would last a lifetime between her and her new brother Brigham. From then on Fanny, at age thirteen, took over watching Briggie as I lay coughing uncontrollably on the bed. I barely ever heard her complain. It amazed me how naturally she took to him. She acted like a proud mother and Briggie responded with enthusiasm. He almost always was attached to her hip, even when she milked the cow.

Despite my sorrow over not having the strength to tend to my newborn, we were blessed. Before my time had come with the baby, John had been to the market. On that day he left at dawn, dew topping the fields, causing the day to sparkle. When he returned, the chill had dissipated into warmth and the sparkle could only be seen in John's eyes.

One glance at him told me that something good had happened, but I also knew that if I inquired about what it was, it would be much longer before I received an answer. John liked to tease that way. Therefore I held my tongue and waited.

But John could not hold back any longer and told me about the great fortune with which our family had been blessed. He had finally purchased a cow from Caleb Murdock. This cow, bless her soul, was not like some that refuse to give the life substance of milk. Instead, she willingly produced as much as our family needed. Actually, we had never seen the likes of her before. That cow put out more milk than I would likely see again. Oh, how we loved the butter, cheese, and cottage cheese that we made from the milk.

We would not learn until after Brigham was born and my illness overtook me again how blessed this cow would be. The milk provided the life-giving nutrients that I was not able to provide. But our cow was an odd one. She would only give her milk to our daughter, Fanny. So my child often had Briggie in one arm and milked the cow with the other, twice a day.

Luckily, Brigham took to the bottle. He was not picky like some of my other babies. He did not seem to mind what we fed him as long as he was fed.

Our hopes and dreams of making a livelihood in Whitingham died as we discovered the ground to be too hard to yield a fruitful crop. There were very few level acres fit for cultivation, and stones were everywhere. Another problem—the length and severity of the winters—proved hard on my health.

John searched elsewhere. He heard of an area that was flatter and cheaper and, once cleared, was producing up to forty bushels an acre. Unheard of! We thought that with those improvements, eeking out an existence might not be as difficult as where we now were. We worked hard cultivating the land, improving the crops, making potash to sell to Canada, and collecting maple syrup to sell for money. Our syrup troughs overflowed that year, allowing us to add to our profits. With our property cleared, it was more valuable. Thus the good Lord blessed us again, and we were able to use the extra money to move on to our next adventure.

Chapter 6

Farewell dear babe, my heart's too much content,
Farewell sweet babe, the pleasure of mine eye,
Farewell fair flower that for a space was lent,
Then ta'en away unto eternity.
Blest babe, why should I once bewail thy fate,
Or sigh thy days so soon were terminate,
Sith thou art settled in an everlasting state.

By nature trees do rot when they are grown,
And plums and apples thoroughly ripe do fall.
And corn and grass are in their season mown,
And time brings down what is both strong and tall.
But plants new set to be eradicate,
And buds new blown to have so short a date,
Is by His hand alone that guides nature and fate.

Anne Bradstreet, *In Memory of My Dear Grandchild
Elizabeth Bradstreet, Who Deceased August, 1665, Being
A year and Half Old*, 1678

Sherburne

$\mathcal{W}$e soon found ourselves packing up the family and making another move. This time we traveled to a primitive town with less civilization than Whitingham, called Sherburne. It was located between the Chenango and the Susquehanna rivers. It was situated in the county of Chenango in the state of New York. The quick access to water made farming much easier. I had hopes our survival would be easier there with the plenitude of wild berries, nuts, and wildlife. With such bounty the place had to offer, we felt the Lord had reached out His hand and called us there, promising a comfortable existence.

So in the spring of 1804, despite the challenges it presented, and despite the fact that I was with child, we moved to Sherburne. We took two wagons, one that we again filled with children and the other with our belongings. We used a team of horses and a yoke of oxen. The first stretch of land we traveled had many bog holes that had to be corduroyed with logs and stumps so we could pass. When we were not corduroying the road, we worried about the steep hills our horses were unable to handle alone. I was much relieved when we hit the Bennington road and a much gentler terrain. The roads were in better condition and we progressed faster. Worried about how hard the first part of the journey had been on me in my condition, and wanting to give my unborn child a fighting chance, I caught rest in the back of the wagon, letting a son or a daughter drive the animals and see to the needs of the younger children.

We turned to the Hudson River. We did not cross the river until we reached the dusty and muddy town of Troy. At Troy we boarded a ferry. After crossing the water we traveled along the gentle terrain of old Indian land. This Mohawk Valley was filled with a multitude of trees, whose coolness I enjoyed wandering through.

We saw many a family, who, along with our own, took the opportunity to cut down trees to make potash. Roads in this area were already forming, and other signs indicated previous travelers moving on to Utica. Heaven knows that part of the journey was dusty and confusing. The forest was so thick with trees that it was hard to determine which way we were to travel. Several times we journeyed down a dirt path to a cabin. When we inquired if the inhabitants had heard of Sherburne, more often than not, they had not. Often we learned we had been going in the wrong direction, lost again because of the density of the trees. The younger children struggled to hold back their tears, not wanting to evoke John's anger. When we finished bouncing our way through that region, we headed southwest, straight for the land that was to be our new home, with the Chenango River close by.

I worried after I talked with the neighbors. We heard tales of bear spottings. I also fought back fear at night when timber wolves took to howling. This caused disturbed sleep for me and most of the members of the family, all but John. I watched John sleep peacefully in the bark shelters we had thrown up, right through the creatures' threatening music. He even slept through the awful screech of the panther. Although I did not like the wolves or the panther noises, I found the hoots of owls soothing, reminding me of when I used to listen to them while sitting near the fire in my childhood.

The children and I grew accustomed to the animal noises as John cleared a spot of land, planted, and harvested enough corn to help maintain us through the winter. In between the harvesting labors, we worked hard on building our family log cabin. Our experience in building so many homes in the past helped to make this one more beautiful and well-put-together.

Another miracle occurred that filled us with joy. It was the arrival of my baby, Louisa. My precious daughter came shortly after we arrived at our new home in September. At harvest, we yeilded corn, a few vegetables, and another beautiful life.

Around this time a fine trapper named Jonathan Frye came into our lives. He put up a trading cabin at the back of our property, and in exchange taught my Brigham the art of trapping and how to study runs and trails. I knew learning these skills would benefit Brigham, but that did not stop me from flinching when he talked of becoming a trapper. A trapper's life was not the type of existence I dreamed for him. Trappers spend months at a time alone. And the dangers—when I think about the dangers, I shudder. The trapper could slip and fall, breaking a leg, and no one would ever know until they smelled the stink of his decaying body or stumbled upon his remains when the spring decided to blossom. Trappers were cold and wet much of the time, which led to illness. I would much rather see my Brigham take a loving wife who would care for him prop-erly and watch the two of them create a happy life with of lots of love, completely devoted to serving God. Plus, I wanted to spend my old days adoring my lively grandchildren. I know this might not be, but if I could have my heart's desire it would be so.

Jonathan Frye taught us many things about this new area. I was fascinated by local Indians, the Iroquois, who were friendly. They had signed a treaty over twelve years earlier, agreeing to live on a reservation. Jonathan also told us about the Chippeway Indians. They were a large group who carried a great deal of prestige. These Indians were civilized and more willing to follow after the way God would have us live. They openly shared the hunting grounds, although they did drive the Iroquois out of some land. They lived in circular dwellings with birch poles spread out around the circle, leaning inward to the center where they would all come together. They had sweathouses, which had a fire in the middle, heating up a pile of stones. They closed the hole in the house and poured water over the coals and steam filled the area. When a person had had enough, he would run and jump into the river or a mound of snow. This, in my opinion, was more civilized behavior than most white folks I know who do not even bath once a week.

Chippeway Indians also wore buckskin clothing, which they bleached white. The women used porcupine quills to decorate their skirts, and the men ran around almost naked when they hunted. I never understood how they could wear so little clothing both in the summer and winter. The winters were cold, and my children and I often grew ill. But these Indians did not seem to get sick. That was a great mystery to me. I hoped someday the missionaries would go to them so they can accept Christ.

When I heard Jonathan Frye talk about these Indians, I knew the Lord had blessed this place with safety for our family. We offered many thankful prayers for being surrounded with kind Indians. I must admit to having a great curiosity about the Indians, but I will not admit to how afraid I actually am of them.

My children grew up as everyone else does, but I somehow did not seem to believe that mine would. Nor did I believe that they would branch out on their own. Despite my reluctance, while we were living in Sherburne my daughters began leaving home for good, or so they and I thought. Somehow I was not prepared for the great loss I would feel. Their absence only compounded my sadness when I looked at my younger children and concluded I may very well be dead before they reach that stage.

The first child to go was Nancy. I could not help but wonder if my tall Nancy left our home so early because of the difficulties of the way we lived. When I took to being sick and in bed, a great deal of responsibility fell on her, and she transformed herself into an invaluable helper. A few times she talked to me about how she did not want to be around her father and his tempers. A deep sadness as big as a gully filled me upon hearing this for both my daughter and my husband. I knew they were missing out on a close relationship with each other that would have been a blessing to both.

It was true that John did have a violent temper. After an outburst I would give the targeted child extra attention. Perhaps I would have them sit on my lap and rock them by the fire, or I would slip them some bread dough to nibble on. I could see that my efforts clearly were not enough to undo the damage when Nancy announced to John and me that she was marrying Daniel Kent.

It is every mother's fear that her children will make an ill choice in marriage. My mother had that fear, and she had to live with her belief that I chose poorly. Now I must live with the fact that Nancy might have chosen the first opportunity that crossed her path in order to flee the hardships of our household. I hoped that was not the case, but I suspected it was. If we had money, slaves, and lived on a big plantation with plenty of food and fine clothing, would Nancy have chosen Daniel Kent to be her husband? Deep within me I knew the answer.

Six months after Nancy left our house, my precious Fanny also left to marry her beau, Robert Carr. Fanny was merely sixteen years old when she decided it was her time to enter into a life of her own. Fanny had a more difficult time leaving than Nancy, and my heart did not worry about her choice as much. Oh, the tears that ran down her face as she held little Briggie, wishing him good-bye. My sweet Brigham cried after Fanny for days.

Having children starting to branch out on their own renews my determination to keep the remaining family together. It is my greatest hope if anything happens to me that they, my children, and my husband, will not be separated.

Moving and having babies filled our days, while the nation was engaged in fervor over "Long Tom," Thomas Jefferson, who became the president after a heated conflict with Aaron Burr in 1800. There was much talk of what would happen to our country when the votes came in, and it was discovered that the votes added up to a tie. The tiebreaker was decided by the House of Representatives. Thomas Jefferson must have been the people's choice, because he won the election again in 1804.

Around this time, I would receive letters from my mother informing me that the nation had grown to three and a half million people, and the land owned by the United States had doubled. My father, always the politician, around this time must have let go of some of his anger about who I married, for he wrote me long dissertations on his feelings about the expanding United States. Father praised Thomas Jefferson up one way and down the other for sending James Monroe to France to buy New Orleans and Florida. Then in 1803 when Monroe returned successful I received newspaper clippings of the big event from my father, and another long note on how the deal came into being and how seven and a half million dollars was a steal for the land.

I disagreed with my father on that, thinking the money would have been better spent paying off the nation's debt. It was a mistake to tell Father this because he wrote back in a letter filled with fervor and facts about how these additional lands were going to make the United States into a powerful nation.

Letters from my mother came in a steady stream. It was hard for her, as it was for me, that we were so far apart. My father, on the other hand, only wrote when there were exciting political happenings. This turned out to be the case when he wrote to me about how Emperor Napoleon had lost more than 24,000 French soldiers on the island of St. Dominique following a slave rebellion. As a result France counter-offered to sell all Louisiana. America agreed to buy all that land for three cents an acre, $15 million total.

Father wrote me again in 1804 when Jefferson sent Lewis and Clark on an expedition to discover the best path to the Pacific ocean, to open fur trading, and to gather as much information about our new expanded land as they could. My father's letters encouraged my sons to pretend to be Lewis and Clark embarking on wild adventures.

After these uplifting letters came, it was disappointing when Father wrote about how the last days were surely at our heels. He believed this because he saw the Pasha of Tripoli declaring war on the United States as the beginning of the worldwide wars talked of in the book of Revelation. This conflict started because the United States would not pay more money for protection against pirates on the seas.

Father also saw potentially disastrous problems arising in the petty fighting that continued among our nation's leaders. For example, on July 11, 1804, Aaron Burr killed Alexander Hamilton in a duel over power. I told my children that the downfall of Israel came about over people fighting for power, like King Saul and David who were in constant turmoil. These men's behavior was shameful. They worried more about petty conerns than about God's will.

In different parts of the world, fighting still continued. Britain and France repeatedly tried to provoke the United States into involvement in their feud, especially by pressuring our men into service. Father would write how it would only be a matter of time before the United States caved in. He had underestimated Thomas Jefferson's leadership ability, however. Jefferson decided to solve the problem by establishing the Embargo Act of 1807, which deterred any vessels from traveling to Europe. This action hurt us in the agricultural markets, making it harder for us to earn a profit. I thought Jefferson made the right decision, although there are many angry people who would disagree with me.

Despite being unable to sell crops to Europe, we continued cultivating the land. These activities prevented us from attending as many church services as we would have liked. John and I felt the great urgency to purify ourselves. When we heard that the notorious Lorenzo Dow would be preaching a mere six miles away, we seized the opportunity to hear him.

The outdoor rally was full of commotion and passion, summoning us to war against sin and the devil. Lorenzo called us to come to Jesus and be saved. A force stirred within me and I could not resist voicing a few, "Hallelujah's." John must have been as moved as I, because I heard "Amens" from him, too. Several of our neighbors even fell to the ground from the power of the experience.

I was glad many of our children attended with us. If they had any unbelief about how awful hell was, they doubted no more after they heard Lorenzo's descriptions. We all were afraid about being in

Satan's grasp, forever burning in eternal torture.

Lorenzo Dow taught us that if we stood behind the towering rail of salvation and declared we wanted salvation, we would be saved. I desired all in my family to be so blessed. In turn each member did as beckoned. Rhoda, who becomes sick with heights, was harder to coax into it than the others, but eventually we were victorious. I was so touched by this occurrence and pleased to have been saved, that when I gave birth to a son three years later I named him Lorenzo Dow.

We moved again in 1807. I was not as troubled about this move, as we did not go very far, only a short distance to a place called Dark Hollow, near Cold Brook, somewhere around three miles southwest of Sherburne. Later, in 1810, we moved to the upper end of Cayuga Lake, to a place called Aureluis. Aureluis was a crude community that was even less developed than Sherburne. In some ways, parting from Sherburne was the hardest move I had to make. The night before we left, I went out alone and climbed to my special rock on the hill. I could overlook the place we had lived in for almost nine years and the surrounding homes of our friends and neighbors. The stars shone brightly and seemed as numerous as the grains of sands on a beach.

This spot had been my sanctuary through many events over the past decade. But none were as devastating as when my daughter died. Nabby caught the dreaded consumption from me. Her frail body lacked the strength to fight against the ravishing brutality of the illness. My only comfort in all this is that she went quickly.

Leaving my precious daughter here has undoubtedly mixed my soul with the land, the grass. Tears sealed my heart in the soil those many long hours I sobbed over my daughter's grave. Nabby's death has cast a shadow over me and my life that I feel I will never escape. I remember the many times I wrapped her in my arms and gave her a gentle kiss, the times she laughed, smiled, and teased her brothers and sisters. But her sparkle dimmed when a cough rattled in her chest. The frequency of the cough hastened as consumption rapidly overtook her petite frame. Panicked, I gave her herbs, cooling rags, concocted herbal formulas. Eventually my desperation grew to the point that I sought the care of a doctor, who immediately put her on laudanum.

When I close my eyes, I see her running down the hill with her hair flying behind her, a smile on her angelic face. Other times I picture her helping her father with the land. She was not one to complain. Often I had the impression as I watched her move that she did not belong in this country, among trees, mountains, and bodies of water. She seemed fit for a different place, a different time.

I comfort myself that the Lord did grant me those eleven years with her. I knew my daughter, her hopes, dreams, and aspirations. That will have to be enough.

Today as I write, my coughing has become so extreme, I have to rest for hours between words. Time is quickly slipping by and I am feeling an increasing urgency to record my story. I hope if the gracious Lord decides to take me that peace would settle in my family members' hearts. I know how extremely difficult it was when we lost Nabby. I watched John. He was silent, stoic, not speaking of his pain. I kept my eye on him, even though I felt as though I had been swallowed up into the very depths of misery. Several times I saw my husband wipe at his brow, and walk out to the mound where Nabby lay. He would kneel at her gravestone, his head lowered, looking like he was praying that her soul had found eternal rest—rest that eluded those left behind.

When I looked into John's eyes those first few days and months—and even as long as a year or two later, I saw the same pain that I experienced. Over time it seemed like that agony died down to a dull ache in the corner of his eyes. The same thing happened to me. The pain was still there, but dormant.

I would hate to leave this life and have that same torment well up within John's soul without me there to share the grief. But whether I live or die, it is in the Lord's hands. All I can do is pray for His mercy and know that if He takes me, His wisdom is greater than mine.

Aureluis was heavily forested, with the hills sloping toward the lake and springs that surprised us when they sprouted off from the main lake. In the midst of the water and trees were meadows, making clearing for the crops less necessary. John and the children immediately set to the backbreaking work that had become a way of life. The children worked hard by his side as they cleared five acres to plant corn.

The winters were bitter cold with temperatures sinking well below zero. We called it a "long cold," as we settled down to shiver for what seemed to be forever. Snow drifted from the sky in one continual downfall. Trees drooped from the heavy weight of white and a sky thick with grayish fog.

Our family nestled inside our cabin, working by the fire, and spending time together, grateful for the shelter from the harsh elements outside. When we had those rare times, I would wish we could linger within the cabin enjoying each other's company, but work needed to be done. Sometimes when the workload seemed easier, the boys grew restless, which led them to gather their gear and venture to the lake to ice fish.

The boys also enjoyed hunting and trapping for furs: mainly weasels, marten, and mink. I remember once the boys returned from hunting. They asked me to look in their knap sacks to see the furs they had gotten. My mind was on other things, when I reached in and pulled out the fur. Something wiggled in my hands.

I looked down to find a rat with long claws and beady eyes. Screaming, I dropped the rodent, my heart beating violently as my boys laughed. Those boys knew that rats displeased me.

Trapping tales filled up the winter nights until spring came anew with the thick fog of snow faded away and the rays of the sun breaking through, warming everything in its path. The sweet smell of spring filled the air. The leaves turned to a vibrant array of colors. Stirrings of happiness and gratitude for this gentle beauty sprang up in my chest. I became more pleased with this land, this spot I called home. As I thought back on the "long cold," I knew that the spirit could get weighed down and heavy, but hope sprang eternal. I likened it to the way sin worked in our life. I told my children that the grasp of Satan could be mighty frightful, and could sink them down low, but once the power of purification came upon them and they knew Jesus, then the eternal hope would rise within their chests. The dark depression would be lifted and remembered no more.

My heart continued to ache through the years for my third daughter, Rhoda, who stayed with my parents. I wrote her as often as I could break away from my chores. To my delight she corresponded back with prose filled with the happenings of the city life. At times there was a sad tone in her words when she wrote about her grandparents. I had a hunch my parents were failing more than Rhoda let on. By the fall of 1809 a different granddaughter agreed to reside at Grandfather's and Grandmother's house, freeing my daughter to return to us.

This news caused great commotion in our home. Everyone contributed to preparations for Rhoda's arrival. Some of my daughters set to work organizing and cleaning the kitchen while the others started baking. While they chattered as they worked, I attended to the laundry. Rhoda would find us clean in appearance. As I scrubbed the fabric, I thought how nice it would be if I had a dress to greet Rhoda in, instead of the same one I had worn when I said good-bye. With this on my mind, I looked up in the horizon and saw two figures approaching.

I stood motionless, unable to breathe as the figures came closer. At last in dawn's light I was able to determine the figures as Rhoda—an older, taller version—and with her the stout old deacon, Abner Morton.

Fanny threw open the cabin door and raced past me, screaming, "Rhoda. Rhoda."

Rhoda laughed as Fanny wrapped her arms around her waist. "Fanny, is that you? My, how much you have grown."

By this time everyone from the house had circled Rhoda, but Brigham hid behind my skirts. Rhoda hugged each person, making her way toward me. "Who is that hiding behind you, Mother?"

"Our little Briggie. He is the baby who came after you left us."

Rhoda smiled at him. He buried his head deeper into my skirt. Rhoda rushed over to him, pulled him away from me and swung Brigham around in a circle. At first Brigham cried, but his distress quickly changed into giggles.

Rhoda was swept into the house to try some of the baked goodies that had been prepared for her. She was sampling the cookies and saying how incredible they were when John entered the room with the boys. They had been out in the fields working.

"Look, Father," Nancy said, "Rhoda being here is like an angel gracing our presence."

"It is indeed," John said before smiling at Rhoda.

For John, it seems the less he says, the more he is feeling. He spoke little about Rhoda's return, but he could not hide his eyes that shone with joy.

Rhoda smiled and laughed as she rejoined our family. Although I could not help noticing that her laughing died down and her smile faded when she looked at me. Her eyes seemed concerned and filled with pain.

Shamed, I would pull away from her gaze with its shocked expression. Her eyes spoke truth to me that no one else said. I had been much affected by my disease. I must have been much reduced from what I once was. The decline had been so gradual, perhaps the others did not notice as much.

Like all angels that have human forms, Rhoda was soon noticed by the young men and they began to court her. When Rhoda was twenty-three years of age, she finally settled on the person she wanted to spend the rest of her days with, a Methodist preacher named John Pourtenous Greene. They married in 1813 in Aurelius, Cayuga County, and stayed close. I wondered if the reason they lived near was at Rhoda's insistence. She worried about me and the younger children. It was nice to have her visit so often, always nursing me and attending to my younger children's needs. They loved it when she came. Those were happy times.

We enjoyed our reunion with Rhoda. She talked almost from the moment she arrived home. She told many stories of the city and of her grandparents. She had also picked up my father's love of politics and she gave speeches almost as lengthy as his. The current subject was what was to be done about England and France raiding our ships, trying to provoke us to get involved in the conflict. On April

17, 1808 the Bayonne Decree was issued by Napoleon Bonaparte. He ordered the seizure of any American vessel that encroached on France, Italy, or the Hanseatic ports, claiming this act supported Thomas Jefferson's Embargo Act.

When Jefferson declined office, that was all we heard about from Rhoda. "Jefferson named Madison to win. Mother, did you know his nickname was 'little Jimmy' and also 'the father of the constitution?' He ran against James Monroe, the candidate backed by the southern 'Old Republicans.'" The Eastern Republicans named George Clinton as their candidate. The Federalist party issued the names Charles Cotesworth and Rufus King. George Clinton won the position to be Madison's vice president when Madison won, and we were treated to a running commentary of the whole situation from Rhoda.

By 1810 the population of our nation had grown to over seven million. In 1811 the public outcry against the raiding of our ships and the constant interference with our trade with other nations grew more intense. Americans were angry over the British Order in Council that prohibited United States ships from entering British ports. The feelings of the nation were shown in the election when the cabinet seats were filled with "War Hawks." These men wanted to fight the British and desired to seize the land of Canada as their own.

Also in the year of 1811, the Indians organized themselves and made ready to make war against us. The Shawnee chief named Tecumseh, and his brother, Tenskwatawa, otherwise known as "The Prophet," declared a holy war on the whites. Colonist fought many battles against them.

In 1812 President Madison did what our country had tried so hard to avoid: he declared war against Great Britain. The battle cry, "Free Trade and Sailors' Rights" was heard throughout the union. I was concerned for what would happen to us individually and as a nation.

At the end of 1812 James Madison was elected president again, defeating the man who stood against war, De Witt Clinton. James Madison was presiding over the nation when, in 1813, American General William Henry Harrison won a battle against the British and the Indians. Tecumseh was killed, which weakened the Indians' position to stand up for their rights.

Several attempts were made by the land-hungry War Hawks to overtake Canada, but they were miserably unsuccessful.

The year 1813 was a busy year for us. Besides Rhoda's marriage, our boy John, Jr. married the lovely Theodosia Kimball. John and Rhoda decided to settle down and start their existence together in the area of Aurelius.

Uprooting my family and moving to another place was something I disliked. I struggled to feel at home when the threat of another move seemed to loom over our household. If I began to trust that the new spot would be a place of permanency where I could sink in my roots, it seemed the next week I would look into John's face and see that itching expression. My heart would sink, for sure enough, he would spend more of his time gazing westward with a deep longing. Not long after, he would begin to talk of having better land, and how rich the people became in easier living conditions. When his talk focused on easier, flatter land, ripe with vegetation and animals, it would not be long before he found property and wanted to move.

Chapter 7

I had eight birds hatched in one nest,
Four cocks there were, and the hens the rest.
I nursed them up with pain and care,
Nor cost, nor labour did I spare,
Till at last they felt their wings,
Mounted the trees, and learned to sing; ...

If birds could weep, then would my tears
Let others know what are my fears
Lest this my brood some harm should catch,
And be surprised for want of watch,
Whilst pecking corn and void of care,
They fall un'wares in folwer's snare,
Or whilst on trees they sit and sing,
Some untoward boy at them do fling,
Or whilst allured with bells and glass,
The net be spread, and caught, alas.
Or lest by lime-twigs they be foiled,
Or by some greedy hawks be spoiled.
O would my young, ye saw my breast,

And knew what thoughts there sadly rest,
Great was my pain when I you bred,
Great was my care when you I fed,
Long did I keep you soft and warm,
And with my wings kept off all harm,
My cares are more and fears than ever,
My throbs such now as 'fore were never.
Alas, my birds, you wisdom want,
Of perils, you are ignorant;
Oft times in grass, on trees, in flight,
Sore accidents on you may light.
O to your safety have an eye,
So happy may you live and die.
Meanwhile my days in tunes I'll spend,
Till my weak lays with me shall end.
In shady woods I'll sit and sing,
And things that past to mind I'll bring.
Once young and pleasant, as are you,
But former toys (no joys) adieu.
My age I will not once lament,
But sing, my time so near is spent.
And from the top bough take my flight
Into a country beyond sight,
Where old ones instantly grow young,
And there with seraphims set song;
No reasons cold, not storms they see;
But spring lasts to eternity.

When each of you shall in your nest
Among your young ones take your rest,
In chirping language, oft them tell,
You had a dam that loved you well.
That did what could be done for young,
And nursed you up till you were strong,
And 'fore she once would let you fly,
She showed you joy and misery;
Taught what was good, and what was ill,
What would save life, and what would kill.
Thus gone, amongst you I may live,
And dead, yet speak, and counsel give:
Farewell, my birds, farewell adieu,
I happy am, if well with you.

Anne Bradstreet, *In Reference to Her Children* 1659

Children

*I*t is natural for a mother to wrestle and fret over the well-being of her offspring. I tried my best to raise my children in a proper fashion. Father above knows the troubles they put me through. I demanded that they live a proper life, honoring God with no foolish indulgence in what the devil surrounds us with, such as the vices of dancing and listening to music, which summon evil into the soul.

I instructed each of my children that reading novels, dancing, and listening to music were all behaviors that would put them on a road away from God. There were rules against the playing of cards and expressions like "Darn it" or "the devil."[9] I reminded them often that they must put on the armor of God and keep themselves clean from such intolerable indecencies.[10]

Instead of allowing my children to waste time on such foolishness, I saw to it that they, both the girls and the boys, had the privilege of picking up brush, rolling logs, digging out roots, and consequently bruising shins, feet, and toes. I also made sure that they learned to make bread, wash the dishes, milk the cows, and make butter.[11] They also chopped down trees such as maple, beech, and hemlock, burned logs, split rails, and repaired numerous fences around the different fields we owned.

Of course, they learned the basic skills of trapping muskrat, fox, beaver, and other such animals. Fishing was a big event for my boys. They loved the water, feeling the tug of the currents. Fish was one of the favorite dinners in our house.

None of the children escaped constant lessons on planting, cultivating, and harvesting crops. They also learned to make Indian webs so we could travel through the snow on foot. Other skills they acquired were how to gee and haw oxen, how to build a root cellar and help raise a house. My children have been to more log-raising parties than there are leaves on a blooming maple tree. I can honestly declare that each of my children learned sufficient skills to be independent and venture out on their own.

Not only did they have proficient abilities, but they learned how to take care of their belongings. If we managed to come across a pair of shoes for one of the children, they carried them to church and back, only wearing them in the Lord's sacred house.

Over and over I urged my children to read the Bible. My favorite saying, which I made sure each and every one of them could quote, was "Read it. Observe its precepts, and apply them to your lives as far as you can."[12] If that was the only concept my children understood and took to heart, I feel my life was well spent.

I have a great love for the Bible. John also has an appreciation for the Holy Book. In our home we use the Bible as the reference on how to rule our children with wisdom. For example, if we had two children with a grievance with each other, they would come to me. True, they might have gone to John, but as he had quite a temper, I was the person they chose. I was the appointed judge of our small kingdom and as it says in Exodus 18:21-23, there needs to be a judge over the people. Holding this sacred position, I had the responsibility to fear God, to be a person of truth, to hate covetousness. I was to bring the great matters to John, but the small matters I would take care of, so the burden on John would not be as heavy.

My job was defined in the Bible, to see that I "justif[ied] the righteous, and condemn[ed] the wicked."[13] Another one of my responsibilities was to see that the consequences were carried out and to make sure the defendant was not harmed.[14] The Law of Moses stated that a person who did the offense would be required to pay back the offender double the amount or more for the suffering he caused his victim.[15] I did enjoy the law found in Deuteronomy 21:20-21. I shared it with my children, who did not find as much pleasure in the fact that to be rebellious to the parents could result in stoning, which meant the community would gather around and throw rocks at the offender until he died.

I did not allow unkind behavior, and if my children saw anyone in need of help they were to be sure to stop and give them assistance.[16] That was the way of Christ. He said, "Inasmuch as ye have done it unto one of the least of these my brethren, ye have done it unto me."[17] I often told my children that when they performed a kind deed to another it was as though Christ Himself stood before them and that was whom they served.

As any parent knows, raising children is not easy, and my house was full. I was lucky to have enough children that the older ones could help take care of the younger ones. I believe the good Lord intended it that way.

Raising children, especially out on the frontier, brings with it many accidents. Fortunately for me and my family, God granted me a gift of healing with herbs. One of the worst accidents was when Joseph cut Phinehas' right hand with an ax. Phinehas was not yet two. Oh, did I pray mightily, believing the good Lord could save Phinehas' hand if it was His will. He, after all, had done much harder feats, healing the sick, and raising the dead.

I treated the injured hand as best I could. The hand eventually was restored to full use and the boys were back into mischief before the wound scabbed over. I made sure the ax was put away and lectured all about not playing with the ax around the babies.

I believe as I look back over the way John and I parented that he was the stricter one. At times I found tenderness in my heart for the children and he did not give in to such feelings. He was solid as steel with them, but he also took the time to explain things, and he always taught them of God. Sometimes he grew too stern, and then I stepped in and reminded him that his fervent behavior might need to be calmed.

Times were always hard on the farms on which we lived. This led me to encourage my sons to find work elsewhere, on surrounding farms, to bring in much-needed money. It was a great blessing that we had healthy sons who were able to offer this service to the family. My boys willingly did what they could. They learned the value of hard work and how to contribute. My girls were not left out. They learned how to work with straw, making both hats and baskets. Oh, the messes we used to make!

I strove to have my children focus heavenward, desiring that they knew where they could turn when hard times beset them. Another one of the desires of my heart was to create good relationships between the children. I longed for them to be close to each other when they grew up. They promised me they would not neglect each other and would help one another as I would do for them if I were near. They do not like it when I talk of death, but I have to make sure everything is in proper order, just in case. I do not want to leave anything to chance. My children laugh at me. They say there was never a time when I have not had things in order and that I have never left anything to chance. Well, I am glad they have an understanding of who I am.

I feel compelled to write a little about my children and the lives they are living. I have already written about Nancy, Fanny, Rhoda, and dearest Nabby, so I will not go on about those children. But I do want to tell about my others. Our oldest son and fourth child, John Jr., joined the Methodist church at fifteen and he still continues to attend faithfully. He has brought great happiness to my husband especially. My husband enjoyed having a male hand to aid in the many tasks. John Jr. responded well to his father and went to great lengths to make his father proud by getting up even before John did and by never complaining.

One of the rewards of being a parent is watching offspring develop to their full potential. This certainly was the case when it came to our Joseph, child number seven. As a boy he displayed a high moral fiber and had a propensity toward religion. Others followed his leadership. It was a natural course for him to become a Methodist preacher, one of the finest.

Joseph held the position in a humble manner, cautious not to abuse his authority as his grandfather constantly warned him. His constitution was one of service, awareness of others, and sensitivity to the stirrings of the spirit within him. He taught quite by second nature as though he was never aware that others were learning from him.

Joseph also paid strict devotion to studying the Word and developing his knowledge of the way the Lord dealt with his people. I heard fine stories about him and how he affected positively the lives of the people in his flock. I was pleased by the way he served the Lord.

Joseph truly carried the weight of the world's sin on his shoulders. I often heard him complaining that "there is not a Bible Christian in the world."[18] The tremendous burden of trying to help others realize that God exists and to live their lives accordingly pressed down on him. He became consumed with this quest, talking for hours on end about how all people had developed their own philosophies and beliefs, and none of them sought to discover the actual views of the Lord for themselves. The hours he spent studying in the Bible seemed to have given him the knowledge of the way God actually operates. He was careful and deliberate about determining the will of God, spending hours on his knees. His devotion and desires were the greatest rewards a mother could receive.

Joseph earned much respect for his careful solemn nature. Many times my other children sought his counsel. I, myself, turned to him, and I believe John did, too, in an indirect way. John would never admit he went to his son for counsel, but he mentioned worries in front of Joseph, and John's eyes turned thoughtful and serious as Joseph elaborated his opinion.

My dear eighth child, Phinehas, also had the love of religion within his soul. He frequently went the Methodist route, but then he started struggling. It was as though he believed in God, but he was not sure of the proper way to worship. He tried this and that, and explored different avenues. This caused me many worries. I could tell the enticements of the world allured him. Despite my best attempts to influence him, he had a taste for them. He was in a tug of war, going back and forth between the Methodist church and the world.

This war over his soul is not ended, and might not be for many years to come. I hope he will grow out of this struggle. Perhaps, in time, he will become more settled with religion and find the one that fits his needs. Until then, he and the welfare of his soul fill up countless hours of my prayers, entreating God to reach out to him and give him the experiences my dear Phinehas needs in order to follow Him faithfully.

Despite the fact that I believe God watches out for Phinehas, I fret that there was more I could have done. Could I have taught him something more? Did I teach him well enough about God and His greatness? What did I do wrong that made his faith incomplete? Was I not strict enough? Too strict? Why does he struggle while my other children do not? These questions have no answers, and they often keep me awake at night.

Although my husband says very little about Phinehas, he also worries. There have been times when he spends an awfully long part of the night on his knees. At least if we must suffer this heartache, John and I do it together. When John climbs into bed after those long prayers, I reach over and take his hand. He squeezes mine, and

we know that together we have petitioned our Maker, who truly
cares for us all.

Our last son, Lorenzo, is perhaps the most devoted to God. He
is soft spoken and meek in nature. I often found him praying, for
he turned early to God to find answers and direction to guide his
life. He repeatedly said our family would play an important part in
the religious movement spreading through the country. I never
knew what to make of that. Our family? And I did not know what
had gotten into him when it came to church activity. He said, self-
assuredly, that a "guardian spirit" told him to join no church. The
way he talked about it, his firmness and unwavering conviction
showed in his decision, so that I was moved to believe him.

I prefer to attend church when my health allows it, but I admire
his character for firmly sticking to God's direction for him. He is
such a lovely boy and hardly could a flaw be found in him.

He had a dream when he was nine that caused me to ponder
upon him, Brigham, and all of us. He wrote it in his journal. I do
not want to mistake, so I will quote it exactly:

> I thought I stood in an open space of ground and saw a good,
> well defined road leading, at an angle of forty-five degrees,
> into the air as far as I could see. I heard a noise similar to that
> of a carriage in rapid motion, at what seemed the upper end
> of the road. In a moment it came into sight, drawn by a pair
> of beautiful white horses. The carriage and harness appeared

brilliant with gold, and the horses traveled with the speed of the wind. It was manifested to me that the Savior was in the carriage, and that it was driven by His servant. It stopped near me and the Savior inquired, "Where is your brother Brigham?" After answering His question He inquired about my other brothers, and concerning my father. His queries being answered satisfactorily, He stated that He wanted us all, but especially my brother Brigham. The team then turned about and returned the way it came . . .

And now to my son, Brigham, our ninth child. I named him after my grandparents on my mother's side. He was not much of a reader, so I did not often find him reading the Bible, but his mind dwelled on God and His mysteries. He talked often to his brothers about his thoughts and theirs. My, they dove into lively conversations late at night when we gathered as a family. Brigham was practical about his view on God. God had to make sense in the everyday life. While his brothers sometimes talked endlessly of God's glory and His mysterious nature, Brigham talked about how God had His hand in his life, sharing experiences which he had in the day that allowed him to know God was actively involved. I remember Brigham boasted that God had granted the gift of discernment to him because often, when he saw a person in the distance, he was able to tell what kind of spirit that person had.[19]

Although Brigham had a religious nature, that did not mean he stood in line and joined a church. He did no such thing. He did not like the doctrines the churches promoted, and he would not join any. It did not matter to Brigham if the priest came to our home and spoke animatedly with him, trying to convince him to comply. He firmly held to his own convictions. Even as young as eight, he stood up to the preachers and their persuasions. When he was older, he explained his position: "I used to think to myself, 'Some one of you may be right, but hold on, wait awhile! When I reach the years of judgment and discretion I can judge for myself; and in the meanwhile I will take no course either with one party or the other.'"[20]

I do not worry about Brigham and the future he will carve out for himself. He has a great longing to find out anything that is the truth about God, heaven, and what we were doing here on earth. This search consumes him. As I would tell him my beliefs, he would shake his head. "But how do you know that, Mother? How do you know for sure? There is not enough answer there."

He has a need for something I do not seem to have the answers for, but he will find them.

Susannah was child number five. She was an interesting girl from the beginning. When she was young, she would join the boys, wanting to cut and saw, and learn how to put things together. It came as no surprise when she chose to marry someone with similar interests. After we moved to Cayuga County and settled into home life there, it did not surprise me much that she decided to marry a fascinating man. The man who captured her heart, James

Little, was a local builder and horticulturist. They live close to us. I have enjoyed seeing them together laughing, smiling, and happy. That is enough to satisfy my heart.

James Little is a bright one. His mind is always going, thinking, figuring out things. I have every confidence that he will do well in carving out an existence in this area and, if my mother hunch is right, he will improve the existence for everyone. He is extremely talented at inventing gadgets, especially those to do with food. He can talk about food, gardening, farming, seeds, and harvest for what seems forever. I must admit, I grow tired of listening to him, but sweet Susannah—either she is completely blinded in love for this Irish man, or she has a complimentary obsession for such matters herself.

Louisa is still a child, not even eight years old. I fear that I will leave her alone in this world if this illness gets the best of me. I know my other children will not let this happen, but having a caring sister, although a very good thing, is not the same as having a mother you can turn to. If a miracle does not happen, it will be Lousia and Lorenzo who will still be young and unready to stand on their own. I regret most leaving the younger children. They will consume my thoughts as I die and, God willing, I will come back as an angel to help raise them. I do not intend to desert my children, not even in death.

RETURNING TO DUST

I lie here restless with fear in a broken sleep,
My blurry sad eyes continue endlessly to weep.
What will my life's loves do, where will they go?
When my life has past, please God let me know.
My frail body is ready and when it dies,
The spirit within will depart with sighs.
One with joy for the relief from agony and pain,
A second of sorrow for my loves I'll not hold again.
As leaves fall in the autumn and return to dust,
Like all living on earth, knowledge says that I must.
Past the cold winter of death lies that of eternity without strife,
Spring will come where loving spirits will find a new life.

Jean Chatwin

ife always has its challenges, and it looks as though the good
Lord is set on me wrestling with sickness, and I willingly submit to whatever ailment my Father in Heaven sees fit to bestow on
me. After all, Job suffered through much harder trials than I, and he

was a mighty prophet of God. I pale in such comparisons. Job did not murmur. I have been purified and saved. The goodness of God is greater in me than the strong powers of the devil that continually try to lay claim on my soul. I do wish I had the necessary strength to help out around the place, especially with the money problems we encountered due to the value of potash sinking to almost nothing. I see the worried, stressed lines on John's face, although he speaks little of it. It is a heavy burden on him, and with me too weak to stand by his side. I pray for him. I long to have the energy I once did, and be a help to my husband instead of being a strain. He never says I am. He never would. But how could I not be? I've heard of husbands who've left their wives' sides if they no longer proved useful. John would never be like that. He loves me, no matter what state I am in. He would much rather I be here, coughing, spitting out bloody sputum, out of breath, and weak, with my lungs burning awfully bad, rarely making it from my bed, than silent and no longer a worry, deep in the rich ground.

John is a true family man. I wonder if the idea of running off and deserting us in our miserable existence has ever crossed his mind. I do not know of him ever wanting to leave us. This speaks for his character. What I do know is that having a family has brought him much happiness. He loves having what he lacked as a child.

He speaks to me sometimes when the rest of the family is settled and asleep in their beds. He talks of when I did have strength. He treasures those times, and so do I. We discuss our courtship and how he caused my heart to flutter in ways I did not think possible. It is like pure energy escaping from my chest, reaching out, calling to him. We explore how our souls connect on a deep, personal level and how the bond expands daily, deepening into something precious and sustaining. We talk about how blessed we are to have known love and to have embraced each other and supported each other through all the hard times. We both accept that life has its challenges—that is the way the good Lord planned. But He gives us goodness if we believe in Him. We believed, and He blessed us to find each other and to experience this love.

My parents did not understand this. They thought I made a mistake marrying John, but I did not. Even if this hard life has caused me to lose my health, even if it means I lost my precious Nabby, even if it means that I was to do back-breaking work for the rest of my life, I am glad that I chose John. Our love is such that I would not have preferred a richer man of prestige, even one with less of a temper.

John and I have eleven children together. Like any proud mother, I must say they are fine, outstanding individuals who will fill honorable places in this life. They know hard work and have inherited the determination of their father. Just as John never gives up, they will not either. There is no obstacle they will encounter that they will not be able to overcome. My house has never been quiet and never lacks for something to do. They filled my life and I hope that in a small way I have filled theirs.

I am in my late forties now. The life that I have lived has aged me quickly. I feel tired and I ache. I do not have the strength that I once did. In my mind, I am as strong as I was at seventeen. In my mind, I am a young girl, hungry for adventure and experience. Strange, is it not? All these years I have lived, I have had many adventures bearing and raising children, finding people and things to love in place after place, yet deep within me I yearn for more.

Despite these youthful yearnings, these past years the thoughts of death have not been far from my mind. I will welcome going back to my Maker. I have few real regrets concerning my life. I have purified myself at every opportunity. I have avoided the evils that plague the world. I have given my best to do good to my husband and children. I have been married now for thirty years. All those years I have done what I could to stand by my husband's side. I would not trade that for anything.

I believe harsh winters brought on my health challenges. As the wind blew the cold against us during those endless days of brief light and a lot of snow and wind, I felt my life seeping from me. I longed for the sunlight and its welcoming healing rays to wash over me.

I am grateful to have the warming truth of God's Word in my life. If I had to do without God's love or His Word or goodness, I surely would have withered away a long time ago. God was truly the light of all our existence and if I must experience the ravages of disease, the bitterness of struggle and disappointment, the harshness of winters to understand how harsh it would be without His warmth and light, then I willingly submit. The lesson was well worth the cost. It is my hope that, as I learned this lesson, my children learned it, too, and that they will not be called upon to go through the same as I did. This wish was not granted to Nabby. She is in God's hands, where I place all my children, as they embark on their lives.

The summers with their heat and humidity were almost as bad as the winters. The ground where we toiled always, always had rocks. I wondered as I worked the ground if the soil was more rocks than dirt. If by some act of God the rocks vanished, there would have been no land there at all. To add to our troubles, we tried to cultivate the land, uneven as it was. In the summer when our chores were done I would watch the children race through the mazes of trees. Fall would come and from those same trees we would labor to pick the fruit. During winter I would stare at the ice covered trees that seemed like ice sculptures. Then the weather changed to the welcoming spring that covered the clusters of trees with vivid blossoms.

Nothing could compare to the beauty of the land that exploded in spring and fall. It was as if God was saying He was sorry He had to put us through those dreadfully long winters and the harsh, melting summers. He gave us this gift to keep us in this area, to keep us dreaming that we might thrive in this wild territory.

As I continue my reflections, I think about how the world has changed since the time I was young. There have been many advances. When I first married John, it was commonplace for everyone, when not working on maintaining the crops and animals, to spend their surplus time taking raw materials and making them into needed items. My, how the children fussed, wanting to play or swim in the nearby pond, but work always came first.

One of the most time consuming tasks was keeping the family clothed. When we were fortunate enough to gather wool, we would spin it into thread, and then weave it slowly into clothing. Now it is more common for those who have the funds to purchase cloth or ready-made clothing from a great city like Boston. That privilege did not come to our family often. Sometimes we would trade for clothing, but more often than not, we had to make the things we wore ourselves.

We also clothed ourselves with articles like coon-skin caps. Those caps kept the sin of vanity out of our house as surely as anything else would because of their lack of appeal. Very rarely did anyone in our family have shoes and, more likely than not, when they did acquire shoes it was not the luxury of boots or actual shoes, but moccasins. We could more easily get the skins to make those.

Another advance that some day I wish to take more advantage of is ready-made furniture. Think of all the time it would save to go to the store and pick out the furniture instead of waiting years sometimes for a piece to be done. The metal spring placed in wagons for greater comfort is an item I have been able to enjoy, although I wish this invention could have come along earlier before the many pregnancies and moves.

Right now there are five of my children living with me still, not yet ready to branch out on their own-Joseph, Phinehas, Brigham, Louisa, and Lorenzo. Their ages range from eighteen to under eight.

At least I have lived long enough to see all of my children raised from infancy to childhood. They are old enough to not need my constant attention. They are all of the age where they can be of service and contribute to sustaining life here on the farm. I do hope that my younger children and husband can stay together. That will make it not as difficult if this disease overcomes me.

I try to offer cheerful, encouraging words to each person in the family when they come through the doors of our home, even when my strength weakens. If I am not caught away by so much pain that I become unaware of my surroundings, I smile to whomever is in the room. I want to lighten their burdens. Also, when my strength is up and the coughing fits do not consume me, I sew and churn. Another thing that I have been capable of doing is reading to my children. They gather around me in my bed and I prop up the Bible and read to them the words of life.

Sometimes when the Spirit moves me, I pull myself out of my bed, put on my traveling clothes, and visit those I feel impressed to see. I make short trips to surrounding neighbors to offer them friendship and support. Every time this happens, there has been an important reason for going. I am blessed from on high to heed His promptings. Service to others makes me stronger. I tell my children about the importance of doing this. I hope they also develop a sense of responsibility to others, and meet others' needs as they would meet their own. This is one of the central concepts of being Christian that so few professed Christians apply to their lives.

I have been much blessed throughout my life to have many choice and good friends. It is a delight when they come calling. The conversation and pleasant laughter take my mind off my struggles and relieve the gloom of an invalid's life.

One thing I especially enjoy doing is talking to newly married couples, advising them on how to start their relationships out on solid ground. I have counseled many young couples in this manner. They seem to enjoy our friendly chats, and I relish seeing the love and the quick flashes of affection that pass between these young couples. I encourage them to keep the love and nurture what they feel for each other, work at it, cherish one another through all life may bring them. I have seen so many people grow unhappy with each other because they become more critical than supportive.

But, despite what I try to do to help keep this family running, my strength fails me. After my girls left in marriage, the full load of housework as well as that of the farm fell on John and my sons. Although it is unorthodox for men to tend to nursing and to do the house maintenance, this act of service has been good for my boys. The boys bake bread, make butter, prepare the meals, clean up the house, and even milk the cows.

When I am too weak to walk, my boys carry me from my bed to the table to eat and then, before they leave for work, one of them returns me to the chair in front of the fire. That way I stay warm throughout the day. As the day draws to a close, my boys come home again, move me from place to place, then set to work to keeping the house in order.

I have seen shifts in their characters through the years as my boys yield their time to caring for me. At first there was resentment and embarrassment in doing what our society tells us is woman's work, but as the years go by and consumption takes over more of my body and drains more of my strength, subtle changes have happened in them. I see compassion in each of my sons' eyes as they come to me and ask how I am doing and how they can best attend to me. They grow in stature and strength as they haul me from my bed to rocker, and realize how essential is their strength, tempered by tenderness.

John is a fine example to them. He has been known to be a harsh man at times, often resorting to hitting before talking, but he never directed that kind of behavior toward me. He is always kind and tender. He lovingly takes care of me. The boys see this. They see the love that exists between us. It touches them. I hope they will treat their wives in much the same gentle fashion. It is, I know, the way God would have it.

Perhaps there is a divine reason in my illness and the fact that I am confined to bed. Perhaps there was a reason why a hard-working and God-fearing man such as John has not risen out of poverty. Perhaps there is a reason why we have to work hard and have been driven to move, and move, and move, in hopes that good fortune will smile upon us. Perhaps, if there is a reason—and I believe with God there is always a reason—I will never know why. Even if I live all my days and never learn that reason, I still put my trust in God and believe that He directs our daily affairs. His will is the way things ought to be.

As God is directing our personal affairs, His hand is also involved in the affairs of government. For example, in the middle of the year of 1814 the English ended their bitter conflict with Napoleon. This allowed Britain to focus on her disagreement with our nation. They came out fighting with a vengeance, burning our capital, the White House, and other political buildings in Washington. Obviously the British did this to get even for what we had done to their Canadian City of York. But revenge never pays, and this action inflamed Americans to stop the English.

The English attacked us several times, but the matter came to a screeching halt when General Andrew Jackson slaughtered his opponents in less than an hour on January 8, 1815. Jackson had already paved a pathway of fame when he halted the war with the Indians by winning a decisive victory in the Creek Indian War in 1814.

While General Andrew Jackson became an overnight national hero, John Adams' son was earning his fame at a slower pace by actively seeking a treaty with Britain. This treaty, which declared the war between America and Britain over, was signed December 24, 1814. Peace at last was coming to the nation.

Unfortunately, peace in family life was not what my second oldest child, Fanny, found in her relationship with her husband. She came home to us a few months ago a broken woman, which in turn broke John's heart and mine. Fanny's husband, Robert, had failed her and gave in to the devil's enticements by pursuing other women. I would much rather have my sweet Fanny under my roof than to be exposed to any more wickedness and pain. It is a shame a man would or could do such a thing to Fanny, who has blessed all in the world with her kind, gentle nature. I will not go into further details concerning my feelings about Robert. It is a most delicate situation upon which to comment my most personal thoughts.

I never have wished such suffering on my cherished daughter. The pain this situation causes my heart, watching my child suffer, is unbearable, but I am grateful that Fanny is here in my time of need. She has become my nurse, and her gentle way with me has been a blessing. Not only has she been good to me as I struggle with this ailment, but she also helps little Lorenzo spend his days, keeping him from knowing what I am suffering. It touches me that I can have my young son protected from the pain of witnessing me leave him. Fanny is truly a godsend, but oh, how I wish she came to me under much different circumstances. I wish I could see her with happiness in her life. She, of anyone I know, deserves the tranquility and comfort of being married to a man who loves her completely and makes her smile.

I have just suffered another rough coughing fit. It seems to fill my whole being with burning fire. I feel so physically weak and worn out. I will soon have to sleep, but I do so desire to write more of my feelings. I want to leave my testimony to my children. I want them to know that God is a very real being in the heavens, that He watches over them and orchestrates their lives. He lives. I hope my children will follow the teachings John and I have tried so hard to teach them. They know to stay away from the appearance of evil. They know to stick close to the good Word and to face any hardship head-on. I also hope I have instilled within their beings my love for them. Let them never doubt my belief in God, and let them never doubt the love I have for each of them.

> Death, be not proud, though some have called thee
> Mighty and dreadful, for thou art not so:
> For those whom thou think'st thou dost overthrow
> Die not, poor Death, nor yet can'st thou kill me,
> From rest and sleep, which but thy pictures be,
> Much pleasure; then from thee much more must flow,
> And soonest our best men with thee do go,
> Rest of their bones, and soul's delivery.
> Thou art slave to fate, chance, kings, and desperate men,
> And dost with poison, war, and sickness dwell,
> And poppy or charms can make us sleep as well
> And better than thy stroke; why swell'st thou then?
> One short sleep past, we wake eternally
> And death shall be no more; Death, thou shalt die.
> John Donne, *Holy Sonnets #10*

Afterword

Abigail Howe Young died June 11, 1815. Her greatest fear upon her death was realized. Her husband was unable to keep the family together. John took Joseph, eighteen, Phinehas, sixteen, and Brigham, fourteen, thirty-five miles away to Sugar Hill in Steuben County. Louisa and Lorenzo, the younger children, were left with Nabby's daughter, Rhoda, and her husband, John Greene, in Aurelius.

Abigail's posterity stayed true to her teachings and faith. Upon being introduced to the gospel, all ten of her living children and their spouses joined the Church of Jesus Christ of Latter-day Saints. John Young married Hannah Brown, a widow, who brought her own children into the family. They were married in Steuben, New York. Both he and his new wife joined the church and moved west with the Saints.

Abigail Howe Young is now the mother of countless posterity who are indebted to her great sacrifice and dedication in raising one of the greatest prophets of God, Brigham Young, who said of his mother: "No better woman ever lived in the world than she was."

Notes

1. "The Religious and Family Background of Brigham Young," p, 289.
2. "The Religious and Family Background of Brigham Young," pp. 289-290.
3. Haven, family meeting of 8 January 1845.
4. Letter Aug 5, 1827.
5. Edwards, Jonathan. "Sinners in the Hands of an Angry God." *Anthology of American Literature Volume 1: Colonial Through Romantic 5th Edition* (New York: Macmilliam Publishing Company 1993).
6. Edwards, Jonathan. "Sinners in the Hands of an Angry God." *Anthology of American Literature Volume 1: Colonial Through Romantic 5th Edition* (New York: Macmilliam Publishing Company 1993).
7. *Mothers of the Prophets*, p. 35.
8. S. Dilworth Young, "Here is Brigham," pp.18-20.
9. Little, "Biography of Lorenzo Dow Young," *Utah Historical Quarterly* 14 (1946): 28.
10. *Journal of Discourses*, 26 vols. (London: Latter-Day Saints' Book Depot, 1854-86), 2:94, 6 February 1853.
11. *Journal of Discourses*, 5:97, 2 August 1857.
12. Esplin, "The Emergence of Brigham Young and the Twelve," p.49.
13. Deuteronomy 25: 1.
14. Deuteronomy 25:2-3.
15. See Deuteronomy 22:19, Exodus 22:4.
16. *Journal of Discourses*, 6:290.
17. St. Matthew 25:40.
18. *Ensign*, August 1980, 54.
19. *Journal of Discourses*, 19:6-7.
20. *Journal of Discourses*, 19:65; 14:112.

References

Arrington, Leonard J. *Brigham Young: American Moses* (New York: Alfred Knopf, 1985)

Arrington, Leonard J. and JoAnn Jolley, "The Faithful Young Family: The Parents, Brothers. And Sisters of Brigham," *Ensign* 10 (August 1980): 52-57

Arrington, Leonard, Susan Arrington Madsen, and Emily Madsen Jones, *Mothers of the Prophets*, (Salt Lake City: Bookcraft, 1987).

Brigham Young: The New York Years (Provo, Utah: Brigham Young University Press, 1982)

Cornwall, Rebecca and Richard F. Palmer, "The Religious and Family Background of Brigham Young," *Brigham Young University Studies* 18 (Spring 1978)

England, Eugene. "Young Brigham," in *Brother Brigham* (Salt Lake City: Bookcraft, 1980).

Esplin, Ronald K. "The Emergence of Brigham Young and the Twelve to Mormon Leadership, 1830-1841" (Ph.D. diss., Brigham Young University, 1981).

Gates, Susa Young. "Mother of the Latter-Day Prophets: Abigail Howe Young," *Juvenile Instructor* 59 (January 1924).

Gates, Susa Young. "Notes on the Young and Howe Families," *Utah Genealogical and Historical Magazine* 11 (January 1920).

Gates, Susa Young and Leah D. Widtsoe, *The Life Story of Brigham Young* (New York: Macmillan, 1930).

Sessions, Gene A. "John Young, Soldier of the Revolution," *Latter-day Patriots: Nine Mormon Families and Their Revolutionary War Heritage* (Salt Lake City: Deseret Book, 1962).

Young, S. Dilworth. "Here Is Brigham": *Brigham Young, the Years to 1844* (Salt Lake City: Bookcraft, 1964).